S0-FEO-262

The World Beyond

The Library on the Other Side

Paul L. Bailey

© Copyright 2005 by Paul L. Bailey

© Copyright 2014 by Paul L. Bailey

First Printing 2005
Second Printing 2014

All rights reserved. Except as permitted under the U.S. Copyright Act of 1976, no part of this publication may be reproduced, distributed, or transmitted in any form or by any means, or stored in a database or retrieval system, without the prior permission of the publisher.

Although based on a recurring dream and interactions with the spirit world, this novel is a work of fiction. The characters, names, incidents, dialogue, locations, and plot are the products of the author's imagination or are used fictitiously.

Any resemblance to actual persons, companies, or events in purely coincidental.

Interior images either created by Easytime Services or compliments of the Stock.Xchng.

ISBN-13: 978-1495313660

ISBN-10:1495313662

Part 1

Chapter 1

I had no idea what today would bring. None of us do. It was a sunny and unseasonably warm Sunday in the middle of November. I awoke when an errant beam of morning sunlight splashed through a tiny gap in the vertical blinds and played across my eyes. Lee was snoring. I reached for him, gave him a kiss, and he shook himself awake.

"Morning," he said yawning.

"Good morning. Did you sleep well?" I asked.

Lee scratched his head and ran thick fingers through his silver flecked coal black hair.

"Yeah, I feel great. You?"

"The sun is out. It looks warm outside," I said.

Lee smiled, placed his hands in front of himself at arms length and made a gesture of revving a motorcycle engine with his right fist. "Want to go for a ride?"

He raised one eyebrow and gave me a lopsided grin. I always chuckled when he did that. It so defined who Lee was – a little serious, a little silly, and a little crazy. I watched as he lifted his upper body with one massive forearm. His muscles flexed and rippled and my eyes followed his every movement working from the top of his body to the point where his midsection met the blankets. Lee turned and looked down at me, his dark brown eyes sparkling. I inched the blankets a little higher, surprised by the chill in the air. He was naked from the waist up and the bright morning sunlight danced on the roughly diamond shaped patch of tiny black hairs on his tightly muscled chest. I took a quiet sudden breath and gently bit my lower lip. My, he looked good. Lee smiled at me in a way that could have meant he indeed was considering a motorcycle ride. Then he placed his index finger on my chin and slowly moved it down my neck to the edge of the covers. I shivered with delight. He hooked his finger under the cover and leisurely inched the covers downward. Lee's smile widened and he set his mouth in a crooked half smile. Now I knew exactly what Mr. Leland Thomas Woods was thinking about, and it had nothing whatsoever to do with a motorcycle. I glanced outside at the early morning sunshine and knew that if we stayed in bed much longer Lee would not get out on the bike today. He loved riding so much that I just could not let him miss it. I quickly scooted a few inches away from him.

"There will be plenty of time for that when the sun has gone down, Mr. Woods," I said.

He reached for me, but before he could grab me I was up and out of bed. He whistled at me as I hurried toward the doorway of our room. At the last second before I left the room, I glanced at him, smiled and winked. Lee shot from the bed and I ran toward the bathroom as he pretended to give chase. I got into the bathroom and hurriedly closed the door. Lee pounded on the door for a moment and then I heard him walk toward the other room.

I loved the way that we still played. Sometimes Lee made me forget that I was the forty-seven year old mother of a college student. He made me feel beautiful, a tale not reflected in the cruel medicine cabinet mirror before me. I looked into the bathroom mirror and frowned. I pulled a single gray hair from my head and ran my long thin fingers through the red tangle of curls looking for more gray. I sighed sadly. I was either going to have to color it or go gray gracefully. I washed my face and dabbed at the smattering of pale freckles that spanned my nose and cheeks. My sparkling light green eyes reflected back at me in the mirror. My nose was a little too long, my face a little too wide, and my lips a little too thin. My one good feature was my eyes.

Lee and I enjoyed a long lazy shower and then began the arduous task of putting on layer after layer of clothing to protect us from the November weather. I went out onto the back deck to feed Wally, our Golden Retriever. Wally was a tall and muscular dog with a sweet disposition. But, I would not have wanted to be at the wrong side of his sharp teeth. From time to time someone would stop by the house that for some reason Wally did not like. He would start barking and growling and showing his teeth. He was very protective of his territory and he could look and sound vicious. Once we had gone away for a week on vacation and left friends to come by and check on Wally. They were going to play with him and make sure he had enough food. We had converted an outside faucet so that Wally could turn it on by licking it so he always had enough water. Wally knew our friends. They had come by several times in the weeks before we left on vacation and spent time with us in the back yard. Wally would play ball with them or simply relax and allow them to pet him. However, when they came by after we had gone away, they met a different Wally. He growled at them so fiercely that they did not dare come into the back yard at all. They edged his food just inside the gate and called to tell us what happened.

Today, Wally was his usual cheery self and wanted me to play ball with him. I threw the ball a couple of times and patted Wally's head. I ran my hands through his magnificent soft coat and told him to have a good day and to protect the house. "By Wally, see you later."

Lee was already backing the big black Road Star motorcycle out of the driveway. He cherished that motorcycle and nicknamed it his Star. He had made a place for it on one side of our two-car garage. The Star sat on a carpet remnant in its stall with motorcycle paraphernalia and a huge stack of toolboxes surrounding it. I had heard Lee brag of the bike's 1600 cc engine so often that although I had no idea what it meant I had caught myself repeating it to my bewildered friends. Sometimes friends would ask me how I could stand the cold weather riding with Lee. I would just smile and say, "Layers, girls. Plenty of warm thick layers!"

To say the least, I practiced what I preached about wearing layers. I walked into the garage wearing a two-piece cobalt blue long underwear set, two pairs of long white tube socks, two pairs of faded blue jeans, a white fleece shirt, and one of Lee's thick flannel winter shirts in checkered and muted shades of green. I still had to put on my heavy leather pants, leather motorcycle jacket, riding boots and thick lined winter-weight leather gloves. I finished dressing by pulling on my white fleece face hood and my burgundy helmet. Lee had the motorcycle warming up at the end of the driveway and he looked so darn sexy dressed in his leathers sitting there ready to ride that I had to chase a bedroom thought from my mind.

Lee was six-feet-two inches tall and weighed two hundred pounds. He had a body built not at the local gymnasium but by the hard physical labor of chopping and stacking cord after cord of mixed wood for our fireplace. I looked at him sitting with his back to me at the end of the driveway and pictured him standing in our back yard with his shirt off, his hair mussed, his muscles tensing and releasing as he swung the ax repeatedly. I thought of the musky scent of his perspiration and I bit my lower lip again. I started to walk down the driveway toward him and he turned to look at me.

"Honey, would you mind grabbing my sunglasses?" Lee asked.

I blew Lee a kiss and turned to go back toward the garage. Lee keeps a small black plastic garage door opener in one of the inside zippered pockets of his motorcycle jacket. He hit the button on the remote and the garage door began to rise. The electric sound of the opener was muted by the contented deep growl of the twin motorcycle engines at idle.

"Can you find the glasses alright, Leena?" Lee asked.

"You always keep them in the top drawer of the motorcycle dresser. I can find them just fine," I answered.

I smiled at Lee. Didn't he know that I knew everything about him? I came out a moment later and I handed him the glasses. Lee grabbed at me, and I jumped back an inch and playfully slapped his hand.

I gave him a hug and stretched myself to my full five-foot-one and one-half inch height. At my height, the half-inch is important, thank you very much.

I climbed aboard the motorcycle and tapped the center of Lee's back to let him know I was ready. Lee slowly pulled out onto our street and headed east. I do not know why, but I always loved to watch the garage door close as we rode away. It is something I had done since I became comfortable on the back of the bike. I imagined the soft thump of the garage door as it met the cement of the driveway and instead listened to the snarl of the engine subside as we reached the first intersection and rolled to a stop. Lee turned onto Ash Street, a four-lane that could take us toward dozens of destinations. We had nowhere in particular to go; we seldom did when we went for a motorcycle ride.

The sunlight was to our back and the tall oaks and cherry trees along the street swayed in the early morning breeze. Evergreens glowed and seemed to shimmer in anticipation of the new day. To our right, a small dirty white dog, no more than a five pound ball of fur, strained at its leash and barked in high pitched squeaks. I smiled at the idea of it getting loose and wondered what it thought it could do about an eight hundred pound motorcycle. Smoke rose lazily from a few puffing chimneys and the large silhouettes of birds, wings spread wide, sailed above us. White billowing clouds spread further and further apart as the sun rose into the heavens. They seemed to be dancing and darting across the open sky. The sound of the motorcycle engine was a joyous sound as if the Star was laughing and rejoicing as the sun shone on its slick black body. It almost seemed that it was happy to be finally free from the cramped garage.

Lee rode cautiously. He often told me that when riding a motorcycle a good rider would check, double-check and then check again before doing anything. It is strange riding on a powerful motorcycle on a cold sunny day. While the sun reached to warm me the cold air and wind rushed by and began to seep through the layers of clothing. If not for the fleece face hood tucked under my helmet and the heat of the motorcycle pipes, the wind might have reached me and made the wind's embrace too cold to enjoy. I hunched my back and slid toward Lee. The wind was mostly blocked now and the feel of his strong body brought me comfort and warmth.

Lee turned toward the entrance to the freeway and I knew immediately where we were going. There was a beautiful back road a few miles north of here and it was perfect for motorcycling. It had rolling green hills dotted with grazing cattle and grassy pastures full of lively horses. Dozens of sheep, their fleece still heavy in the winter sun, would wander peacefully together through an unmarked pathway of curves that only they could see. There was usually almost no car traffic at all on the back road and Lee loved to let the big Yamaha purr through the straight sections. Then he would use the powerful engine to pull us free of the twist of one curve and into the cramped horseshoe of the next.

It was about six miles up the freeway to the exit and since I had never particularly enjoyed riding on the freeway on the motorcycle, I spent my time thinking. That day, I was thinking about our twenty-one year old daughter

Sara, and wondering just what sort of trouble she might be getting herself into after three years at college all the way in Maine. Sara would gather the attention of many of the college boys with her long straight raven hair, russet brown eyes and tall thin body. Sara took after her father. She was beautiful, graceful and full of joyous energy and a zeal for life. I smiled just thinking of her. A moment passed and I remembered that I needed to get a birthday card for my brother Alan. How old was he now? Forty-nine I thought. My, how time flies. I wondered if he would ever get his act together. Sometimes I thought Sara's best friend's little children had more sense than Alan did. I thought of my own father; Roy Melvin, and how when I was a little girl I had loved to run into his big arms when he got home from work. Papa had been a laborer. Some called him unskilled, but I saw the miraculous things he created with his hands. How could an unskilled man create such wonderful things?

That brought me to a thought of our son Seth. Seth had taken after me with his light strawberry blond hair and relatively short stature. His manly, yet boyish good looks had turned the heads of many young ladies. Seth had been a handsome, sometimes lighthearted and sometimes scary boy. I wondered if he would be out here riding with us today if he had just called in sick instead of going to work that April Saturday morning four years ago. The boy had been a daredevil and believed that he was indestructible. He was a superman in his own mind and he never bothered to look where he was going. He would laugh and tell of time after time of almost being hit by a car, coming close to falling from some high crag, or nearly suffering some other terrible fate. The silly boy had been crossing a busy street in heavy traffic on a rainy fog blanketed day. He must have known that the view of drivers would be limited in that kind of weather. Nevertheless, he was unlikely to be paying attention to where he was going. He seemed certain that nothing could harm him. He believed that the most that could happen would be that he would have another amusing tale to brag about. I am not sure he ever saw the bus that hit him as he tried to cross the street.

I had never felt such a horrible and empty feeling in my life as the day I had to call Lee and tell him the horrible news. I had arrived home from work and a black-and-white police car was sitting in front of our house. The officer had slowly unfolded himself from his car and walked toward me with his eyes downcast. In that moment I knew that he bore no news I would want to hear. The officer's badge glinted in the passing rays of sunlight and he spoke in a soft sorrowful tone. He told me that a bus had hit Seth and that our beautiful son was gone. Seth had been only twenty years old. It was all just too much. I tossed my head and opened my face shield a notch to wipe away my tears and allowed the cold wind to wash the memory away. The wind's late fall chill stung my face and took my breath away. I gathered my scattered thoughts and looked around. I thought to myself, "Oh good, the exit is coming up," then I saw Lee turn on his right turn signal and glance into the right side view mirror.

Something was wrong. The brake lights on the car in front of us quickly came on and glowed. The car was quickly reducing its speed. Instinctively, I closed my face shield and tried to ready myself. I felt the motorcycle accelerate as Lee turned away from the mirror and then saw him flinch as he recognized that the car in front of us was much too close. As if in slow motion, I watched in horror as it all happened. Lee hit the brakes and I heard them start to squeal. It was the sound of a throng of sad birds crying in unison, shrill and piercing. That sound died and the thudding of the heavily breathing decelerating twin motorcycle engines replaced it. The sun glinted on the rear windshield of the white car in front of us, as it grew closer. Something hit the back of the motorcycle and I lost my grip on Lee. I heard the scraping of the bike's engine guards as they hit the pavement and the sickening sound of crunching metal. I felt myself being thrown up into the air and the next thing I knew I could feel nothing at all. All I could see was a close up view of perhaps twelve square inches of pavement. I had never noticed the color and size variations of the pebbles in the pavement before, or how they glow in the sunlight. It was almost like viewing a dozen dazzling diamonds in my favorite Tiffany & Co. jeweler's case.

A crowd began to gather from nowhere. Sirens were wailing, first further away, then closer – and closer still. People were chattering at me screaming meaningless words in a dizzying flurry of motions and colors and sounds. I could hear every word but somehow none of it had meaning. It was like awakening to find myself in a foreign country whose language I had never heard. Everyone around me was speaking more loudly than necessary as if the increased volume would help to convey the meaning of the words.

Where was Lee? Oh, God! Where was Lee?

The sound altered and someone yelled something I understood.

"Sit down," Someone yelled. "Sit down, sir," another yelled.

The sirens were closer and I felt the rhythm of their sound vibrating through my body. Someone was checking my pulse. A string of unintelligible medical gibberish came from numerous disembodied voices. Someone moved my legs and white-hot pain shot through my body. I felt as if I were going to pass out and would have welcomed it if it were to ebb the excruciating pain. I could hear the blaring siren and sense the jostling of the ambulance as it raced toward the hospital. I heard two voices; one male, one female, exchanging medical terminology. Every minute or so I could see an out of focus face block the light and a female voice would ask, "Mrs. Wood, can you hear me Mrs. Wood."

I wanted to tell her that I could hear her just fine and that the name was Woods, not Wood, but I could not get my mouth to move. I wanted to ask for a blanket, I was so cold. I wanted to ask for something for the pain, it was unbearable. But, no sound would come and none of my body would move.

"Mrs. Wood?" she tried again. "Mrs. Wood – can you lift your hand?"

I tried, but I could not.

"Mrs. Wood, can you lift your hand?" she asked more loudly.

I simply could not move. I could not speak. I became frightened.

The ambulance attendant gave up trying to talk to me and I heard people talking on a metallic sounding radio that compressed their voices and gave them a near cartoon character quality. Someone put a warm blanket over me and I began to relax. They must have given me something for the pain too, because the ride was now more tolerable. I sensed the rhythmic almost melodious rise and fall of the siren and the rattling, jostling and vibrating of the ambulance. A curve led to a rocking motion and my body strained against the straps that restrained me. Then the ambulance gave a final quiver and came to a stop. The door at my feet swung open and someone rolled me out of the ambulance and into the red stained light of the emergency rooms neon sign. A person on each side of me lifted me onto a table and someone pushed me into the hospital's emergency room.

Orchestrated chaos was the only way to describe what happened in the next few moments. Someone rolled me into to a tiny room filled with bright lights. People were coming, going, shouting and prodding me. Strange machines and medical contraptions were everywhere. I lay there wondering if Lee was here somewhere and if he was going to be all right. A man with a practiced calm in his voice spoke to me. He described each medical procedure just before he began them and I instinctively trusted him. Then someone moved my legs again. Unimaginable searing and tearing pain tore through my body. It was a pain beyond childbirth or any other agony that I had ever endured. A drape of darkness fell around me and reality began to dissolve. Everything went black and still.

Chapter 2

Then, the strangest thing happened. I felt myself floating and rising to the ceiling until I hovered in one corner of the room. I could see the entire room below me. A woman's middle-aged body was lying on a hospital rolling table. Her long red hair had more gray than I thought mine had and she looked as if she could stand to lose ten pounds, but her face was the face I had seen in the mirror this morning. Two doctors and three nurses were working around my body.

"She's lost consciousness. Notify ICU and get a neurosurgeon down here stat. There is nothing more that we can do here," a tall dark skinned doctor said.

"Give me a minute Doctor Lane," the shorter doctor said.

The shorter doctor was the one with a practiced calm in his voice. He worked feverishly over my body and seemed determined to find a way to heal me.

"Doctor Pritchard, she's not going to ….." Dr. Lane said.

Sweat formed on the brow of Dr. Pritchard's pale pink forehead. He continued working over my body without looking up. He connected some sort of electrical medical device to my body and did test after test to evaluate my condition.

"Doctor Pritchard! Let's leave it to the neurosurgeon, maybe there is something he can do," Dr. Lane said more firmly.

Dr. Pritchard glanced up at Dr. Lane with a look of disgust. Then he looked back toward my body and sighed. I looked down at my body lying on the table and it looked cramped, old and worn. I was floating up here in the corner of the room – able to see and hear everything. I felt no pain and no pressure. I was no longer cold or uncomfortable. I felt strangely detached from the scene playing out below me. From my viewpoint it was a little like watching an episode of medical show on television. The actors were doing a good job of playing their parts, but I kept wondering when the story would be interrupted and a car company would tell of its new low-interest financing offer or a drug company would suggest everyone call their doctor about a new prescription medicine.

A young nurse's aide came through the door and asked, "Her husband is in observation. Can he see her?"

'Thank God, he is all right,' I thought.

Dr. Lane glared at Dr. Pritchard and spoke again. I was now certain that Dr. Lane was in charge.

"We have a closed head injury here. The patient has suffered severe trauma and lost consciousness. Move her to observation and monitor her for brain swelling. Maybe the best thing we can do is let her family spend some time with her," Dr. Lane said.

Dr. Pritchard looked disappointed and he left the room with his kind blue eyes downcast. I thought I saw the glint of a tear on his face. I watched and listened as the room quickly emptied and quiet was restored.

I floated along the acoustic tiled ceiling while an aide pushed a rolling bed that contained my body up a wide hall with highly polished floors. He rolled my body into an observation room and I settled into the left front corner of the rooms ceiling. In a moment or two, a short, thin, balding man wearing thick glasses and a white lab coat entered the room. He raised each of the eyelids of my body and shown a flashlight in each eye. He opened a metal colored file holder and scribbled furiously and then allowed the file holder to fall and clang on the side of the bed. He looked at my body, gave a dismissive shrug and hurried away without saying a word. A moment later a heavier black haired man in a blue lab coat pushed Lee into the room. It seemed so strange seeing Lee in a wheel chair.

"Oh Leena…." Lee said.

The man in the lab coat interrupted Lee and said, "I'm afraid she is unconscious, Mr. Woods. She cannot hear you and she won't even know you are here."

Lee turned toward my body. "Honey?" he asked.

"Your wife is unconscious Mr. Woods," lab coat man said with cold impatience.

I wanted to let Lee know that I could hear him. I wanted him to know that I was here hovering near the ceiling in the rooms left corner and not in the broken body he was looking at. I felt myself start to drift toward Lee but the drifting freighted me and I let myself glide back into my corner.

Lee's brown eyes became cold steel as he looked up at the man in the lab coat.

"I intend to speak to her," Lee spoke each word separately, distinctly and in a tone that I seldom heard Lee employ. Lee spoke in moderate volume but the anger in his voice was palpable. He looked violent and I had not realized that he could become so angry with anyone. The man in the lab coat looked at him condescendingly, smirked, gave a mirthless honk of a laugh and strode from the room. I wished that I could move my body. I would get up and give the insolent idiot a piece of my mind!

"Honey – can you hear me?" Lee asked.

Of course I could hear him -- but I had no voice to answer him.

"Okay," he said, "I'm going to pretend that you can hear me, there is a lot I need to tell you and I'm not sure how long they will let me stay here," Lee said. "Honey, I am so sorry!" he said with tears in his eyes.

Then he paused, turned away from my body and cleared his throat. He wiped his eyes and turned back toward me. He put an overly cheerful tone in his voice and forced his face to pretend to smile. The result was more frightening than seeing his tears. Lee's forced smile did not reach his bloodshot eyes. His hair was in disarray and worry and grief were etched deep in the lines of his forehead. It was then that I understood that the doctors must have told Lee that I would not live.

Lee continued. "A nurse helped me and I called Sara. She is going to catch the first flight out. I called your parents and they are on their way here. Alan will be here when he gets off work and Pastor Rick is coming too," Lee paused for a moment. "Honey, you need to know what happened. We were riding along and I saw the off ramp. I checked the side view to see if we could safely exit but there was a car blocking us there. The guy behind us was speeding up so I goosed the Star and looked forward. By then the car in front of us was almost stopped. I checked everywhere but there was nowhere to go. I hit the brakes hard and then the guy in back of us hit us," he said. Lee stopped talking and he took my body's right hand.

I wished that I could feel his touch and immediately I sensed his touch deep within me. It was like feeling a coin through a thick pair of gloves. The feeling was almost there, but not quite. I started moving toward Lee again, and again I stopped myself. It felt good to have Lee here with me, even if he was holding a hand that was no longer my own. But, moving like that frightened me.

"The Star twisted and I felt it start to go down. I think I was out for a few minutes after the collision. When I came to, I looked around and I didn't see you. I was worried," Lee said. He stroked my body's forehead with his other hand and let his fingers trail down my body's cheek. "My leg was hurting a bit and I had some difficulty getting to my feet. I noticed a commotion in front of the car that we hit so I pulled myself up and I grabbed hold of the car and kept moving until I saw you lying on the pavement," Lee said. "They kept yelling for me to sit down, my leg gave out, and I just sat there looking at you. After they brought us to the hospital, they told me that you were in the next emergency room. They told me you were alive but they would tell me nothing more," he said. Lee turned away to wipe another tear from his eyes and now he spoke in a choked whisper. "You came down in a heap. Your legs were twisted one direction and your body was twisted the other. Your head was bleeding when the paramedic removed your helmet," he said. Lee was still wearing his faded green hospital gown and a blue temporary cast covered his right leg. More bandages covered most of his left leg and right arm. There were tears in his eyes and I wished that I could reach out to him and tell him that I love him. I wished that I could tell him that this was not his fault. Immediately I was beside him and this time I had felt no motion at all. I was near him, but I had no hands to touch him. I had no means to hold him. I was simply there. At this revelation I felt myself rise again and hover in the corner.

Later, my parents entered the hospital room. Mother looked at the room and came to the side opposite of where Lee was sitting. She was wearing a pale pink dress with a white scarf and carrying a large white purse. Her coiffured Clairol blond hair bounced and her short white healed shoes clicked softly on the tile floor as she walked. Mother's makeup was done perfectly and she looked younger than her seventy-one years. Mother took my body's hand and gently caressed my body's forehead. Papa stopped and stood at the foot of the bed as if incapable of moving any further. Papa looked tired and worn and even older than his seventy-four years. His few remaining strands of hair were mussed and his well-worn denim jeans and green-checkered hunting shirt looked a size too big for him. Papa's wallet was in his left shirt pocket and a small hole in his shirt displayed the bottom corner of the brown leather wallet.

Lee called to him and Papa lumbered head down, to a spot next to Lee's wheelchair. Papa touched my body's bandaged arm and moved his big rough hands over the bandaged skin. It was amazing to see those big strong, scarred hands, now liver spotted, move so gently. Father was a man of Lee's height a few years ago but now he seemed to have visibly shrunken. Lee shared an abbreviated version of how the accident had happened and mother and father both listened attentively. When Lee was finished, my father looked up for the first time. His grey eyes glistened sorrowfully as he spoke.

"Lee, and Leena, if you can hear me, Mother and I spoke with one of the officers that was at the scene of the accident. It seems the gentleman in the car behind you suffered a stroke and he accidentally hit the accelerator and collided with the rear of your motorcycle. He passed away an hour ago from complication of the stroke," Papa said looking at Lee. Lee only nodded.

"The driver of the car in front of you saw a kitten trying to cross the freeway and slowed without checking her mirrors. The driver and her passenger, a woman and her son are in the hospital, but they will soon be released. They suffered whiplash and some minor cuts and scrapes." Papa paused again and this time looked toward my body. Although floating five feet above and to the left of where he looked, I found myself trying to nod. As if he understood that I had responded, Papa continued. "Lee, you came off the motorcycle, slid under the rear of the car and came out on the right side of the car that you hit. The best the police can figure, you came out about halfway between the front and the rear tires. It's a good thing you came off the bike, Lee," Papa said.

Lee looked up at him with a cold curious stare and Papa quietly continued.

"The car that hit your motorcycle pushed it part way under the car that that you hit. The car that had been behind you, collided with the car that had been in front of you. You would have been killed if you hadn't come off the bike." Papa looked toward Lee again and Lee nodded again. "The vehicle that was in the exit lane when you checked saw you check and sped up so that you could get over. He was the only vehicle in the exit lane so when you slid under the car and came out the exit lane was clear for you. Leena, the car in front of you came to a complete stop as you were flying over it. The officer said that is the only reason it didn't run you over and kill you on the spot." Papa finished.

It was silent in the hospital room for a while. Then Papa stroked my body's arm again and nodded to Lee and to my body. Papa turned toward Mother and said, "Lynn, I'll be right back. Stay here."

He walked from the room and someone brought Mother a chair. She sat down next to the hospital bed, put on her glasses, and began knitting. Lee sat talking to me and reminded me of some of the good times that we had together.

"Do you remember the tiny wedding chapel where we were married? It wasn't much bigger than this hospital room. There wasn't even an aisle for you to walk. We just sort of stood a few feet from the door and listened to scratchy recorded organ music as the minister went through a two-minute version of the vows," Lee said quietly. The smile on his face now was real, as he himself

The World Beyond: The Library on the Other Side

must have been remembering. "Oh, and you must remember the day Seth was born. How we rushed to the hospital only to wait for hours on end before anything happened. Sara was just the opposite, we almost didn't make it to the hospital and she was practically born in the elevator on the way up to the delivery room. Do you remember how the children cajoled you and me into letting them get a puppy? They both swore they would take care of the dog. Of course, you ended up having to take care of the dog. I was on the road a lot when the kids were little. I was working for Crown Paper as a traveling salesperson. Every time I came home, it seemed that Seth and Sara had grown another inch. They seemed to be arguing about something every time I saw them. I sometimes wonder how you put up with their constant hostility," Lee said. "By the time Seth was twelve years old no one dared lay a hand on Sara. If Seth didn't like a boy that was paying attention to Sara, the boy better either stop paying attention to her or prepare to be pummeled. Then there was that terrible day when we got the news that Seth had been killed. I owe you and Seth both an apology, Leena. I was so angry with Seth for not being more careful that I didn't really morn for him. I allowed myself to focus on my anger, and I'm afraid I didn't help you grieve either," Lee said.

After a moment of silence my mother looked up from her knitting and spoke. "I remember the day you were born, Leena," Mother said. "You were a miracle child. First, the doctor found that the umbilical cord had become wrapped around your neck. They had to struggle just to bring you into this world. Then when you were seven

22

years old, you walked right through a plate glass window and somehow you escaped with only a few cuts and scrapes. I could not have taken it if you had died as a child. After all, it had been such a short time before that your brother David died of that terrible cancer," Mother said.

Pastor Rick Young arrived and prayed for both Lee and me. Pastor was a small man dressed in an inexpensive black suit and carrying a huge Bible with a symbol of a white dove on the blue leather cover. A large silver cross, hung from a heavy silver chain around his neck. "Lee, the church loves both you and Leena and we will be here to help you in any way that we can. The children in the Sunday school class that you teach are praying for you, Leena. The women's group remembers how you helped others and they are going to be bringing Lee meals while you are here in the hospital. We believe that with God's help you can have a complete recovery, Leena," Pastor said. He said another prayer and read a few verses from his Bible aloud. Then he excused himself and left to visit someone else.

The telephone in the room began to ring and Mother got up from her chair to answer it. "It's Sara," mother said, "She wants to talk to you, Leena," Mother held the telephone to the ear of the body on the bed and I allowed myself to float close enough to hear.

Sara said that she loved me and that she had missed me while she had been away at college. She told me about a few of the things that had been happening in her life and then she finished the conversation by telling me she was on her way to the hospital. I floated back up into my corner and saw my brother Alan enter the room. Alan was a gaunt, mendacious, and cruel man. His decades old toupee was dirty and slightly out of place. His mismatched clothing looked as if he had slept in it and his face was dirty and flush with the look of a heavy drinker. Alan was drunk. He staggered into the room and started toward Lee. Mother lifted the receiver, heard the dial tone and put the telephone away.

"You sorry no good son-of-a- ..." Alan started at the top of his voice.

"Alan!" Mother exclaimed. "Watch your language!"

Alan turned toward Mother and argued. "He got Leena hurt on that dumb motorized skateboard of his! It's not enough that he bust up his own sorry leg, he has to put Leena in a co-co coma," Alan sputtered. Alan's face flushed an even angrier shade of scarlet and the veins in his neck and face throbbed. He started toward Lee again.

Papa evidently heard the shouting and came back into the room looking robust and angrier than I have ever seen him. Suddenly Papa's appearance of having shrunk vanished and he moved swiftly and with purpose. He grabbed Alan's arm, spun him around, then seized the back of Alan's shirt and nearly threw him from the room. "Do not come back here unless you are sober and ready to apologize," Papa yelled.

The room was silent for a while. Later, from the hall, I heard the sound of children laughing. It was a sound so full of cheer that it warmed my soul. Sara, her best friend Macy Boyce and Macy's two small children Danny and Marie came through the door. Mother got up from her chair and she and father left for a while and Lee told the story of the accident again. Sara sat in the chair where

Mother had been sitting and Lee kissed my body's hand and wheeled himself from the room so that Macy and the children could gather around the bedside.

"I've got a new dress," said Marie. She spoke the words with a combination of wonder, awe and joy. Her crisp bell sharp tone and simple truthfulness reminded me of childhood innocence. The five year old turned in a complete circle showing off her beautiful new blue and white chiffon dress. Her golden hair sparkled and bounced as she turned. She was missing her front two teeth and her smile was infectious. The sight of her softened the expressions of every person in the room. I even noticed a few smiles.

Not to be outdone, Danny spoke. "Mama's gettin' me a new truck." Danny was six. He towered over tiny Marie and drew himself even taller in his pride. He looked quite the little man in his navy blue dress suit, white shirt, red necktie and short-cropped blond haircut. Macy smiled at the children and at Sara and then led the children from the room. When the children had gone, Lee rolled himself back into the room.

"Hi Momma, I hope you get well soon. Dad and I need you," Sara said. Sara looked at Lee and Lee smiled.

"It's OK, Sara. She's still your mother. Just talk to her like you always have," he said.

"Mom, remember how I used to call you at work all the time? I remember I called you once because a bird flew into the sliding glass door and was hurt. And there was the time that I called you because there was a mouse on the porch and I was afraid to go outside until you came home and scared it away," Sara said. She talked for a while about more of her childhood memories and soon everyone but Macy and the children were back in the room.

A moment later, I noticed someone hovering in the corner beside me. I am certain that I had never seen her before but somehow I knew her. She was clothed in a hooded one-piece robe of pure light. Her face was the only part of her body that I could see, yet I recognized her. Her huge silver eyes shone and her face glowed in the reflection of the light that surrounded her.

"Hello Joan," I said in a language of thought.

"Hello Leena. Do you know why I am here?" Joan communicated back in the same language.

"No," I lied. I did know, but I did not want to know.

Joan smiled. 'It's time, Leena.'

"No! I have to say something to Lee first," I demanded.

Joan looked at me with patience and understanding. "I'll help," she conveyed.

I felt myself fall rapidly toward my body and then I was back inside the body. The terrible throbbing and burning pain returned and my inability to move returned. I looked and saw Joan near my side. I knew that I was the only one in the room able to see her. She slid an arm beneath my back and raised me to a sitting position.

"Look," Lee cried excitedly. He was pointing a finger at me and a genuine smile was forming on his face. "She's sitting up!" he said.

Joan moved my head so that it looked as if I was looking Lee in the eye. Then Joan turned my head so that it looked as if I were looking at each other person in the room. There was a commotion of confusion in the room.

Papa hit the emergency call button for a nurse and everyone else seemed to freeze for a moment in shock and disbelief. Joan opened my mouth and forced one word from my battered body.

"Love," I said.

Joan let my body lay back down and moved my head so that it was straight. I saw a nurse hurry into the room and then I saw a dark spiral tunnel appear in front of me. A very bright light was at the far end of the tunnel and I felt myself move up the tunnel and rapidly away.

Chapter 3

I awoke a moment later and found myself standing in the most stunningly gorgeous garden. The grass was the deepest green the sky the brightest blue. Thousands of fabulous flowers glimmered with most concentrated colors and fragrances. There were roses in hundreds of colors and variations. The roses were soft and sweet smelling and they were in all in full bloom. Beyond the field of roses were gladiolus, kangaroo paw, bird of paradise, lilies, tulips, daisies, carnations and hundreds of varieties of flowers that I had never seen before. Each was more beautiful than the next. The greenery glowed with intensity and enhanced the beauty of the garden. The sight left me breathlessly exhilarated in its simple natural splendor.

Slowly, the most magnificent music began to bubble from the scent of the flowers and the bubbles breezed through the air reminding me of a schoolyard of children playing with small colorful bottles and plastic wands. There were innumerable bubbles and they exploded into countless beautiful butterflies each with wings ridged by sparkling diamonds. The butterflies raced through the sky in a concert of color amid a symphony of sound. Light reflected from the diamond wings and sprayed a dizzying array of tiny spotlights to accent the already stunning flowers.

Clouds of pure white looked like comfortable pillows dotting the sky. Paths of diamonds, sapphires and emeralds wandered through the garden at every angle. I had the feeling I could spend a year, maybe more just exploring the garden and all the beauty that was here. This garden was the essence of serenity. No Earthly garden could ever compare with this, but even now, even here, even before meeting with anyone or anything, I knew that I was no longer on Earth. I was in a world beyond.

A path of gold unfurled beneath my feet and rolled out before me like a carpet. It rolled into the distance and as it did even more flowers flowed into the spaces on either side of the golden path. I took a step and stopped and turned around in a full circle amazed by the bountiful beauty. A bird, yellow and blue and as dainty as can be descended from the sky and landed upon my hand. It looked up at me and I could have sworn that it winked. The bird sang a lovely song and the music of the butterflies worked with the bird's song to create melody and harmony, point and counterpoint. The bird rose from my hand and flew a few feet in front of me and then turned to look at me. It was as if the bird was beckoning me to come and I began to walk.

The gentle rolling hills and winding golden path led me on and on through the intense stunning glory of the garden. The air was warm and a gentle breeze caressed my face and hair. It felt like a breeze but it did not blow on me, but rather flowed through me and danced inside of me. A peaceful pond was to my left and large golden fish were swimming in it, and strangely enough, above it. A frog croaked and its sound was similar to words. It was as if the frog said, "Be not amazed at what you have created." I looked toward the frog in wonder but it was apparently once again only a frog sitting upon a profoundly green mossy stool in the center of the pond.

Joan appeared at my right side and the experience reminded me of a thousand dreams on countless nights on Earth. Joan smiled and a set of silver stars sparkled in the still blue daylight sky. A beam of intense light was approaching from my left and another from my right. The closer the lights came the more I could see that within the intensity of the light were the characteristics of angels. Yet, it was as if the angels were both underexposed photographic images in that they were one with the light and yet separate and distinct from the light. Although the angels seemed far from me when I first noticed them, it took them only a fraction of a second to close the distance and now they stood before me. Each was tall, one was male the other female. Each had a glorious expanse of wings that were the whitest of whites. The wings seemed to be made of the same material as the clouds. I thought of sinking into the softness of the wings as I once sank into the softness of a plush bed pillow.

The angels were dressed in white robes each tied with a single gold sash. They opened their mouths and the most glorious music burst forth. In an instant the music of the butterflies became a chorus of quiet piccolos playing to the entire string section of a huge orchestra. The music washed over me and through me and I felt rested and purified by its range of tones from the deepest of bass notes to the highest peaks of the sound spectrum. The music's vibrations moved through me and reminded me of the constant beating of my heart in the human body I had recently vacated.

I saw a third shaft of light. This light was far brighter than the first two. This light did not move toward me; but in the twinkling of an eye, I moved towards the light. The light did not speak but it shone through me and communicated to me nonetheless. I knew that I was loved by the light and that I was a child of the light. I understood that the light was deity and humility combined in love. The light merged with me and in that moment I experienced an electric ecstasy unlike any other I have ever known. I knew that I was a part of its eternal glory. The angels to my left and to my right also merged into me and through me and in that moment I understood love as I had never before. I knew that what is called love on Earth is a distant, poor, out of focus image of the real thing and I longed to share the reality of love with others.

I felt as if I expanded, not in size, shape or dimension, but with capability and power. It was a feeling of growth and reminded me of my graduation from college in its sense of accomplishment.

I smiled, and then, as quickly as the lights had come, they moved away from me and merged into a light so bright that I had to turn my eyes away. Now the lights were out of my view but I knew they would never truly be gone from me, I understood that they were a part of me and always had been.

The butterflies appeared around me again sparkling, twinkling and rejoicing in blissful laughter. I moved on along the golden path until I rested in the softness of a cloud. I nestled into the smoothness of the clouds comfort and was warmed by the love that surrounded me. Then an exquisite pink flower grew until it reached my ear and it whispered a message to me to be of good cheer. I knew that this garden was only the beginning of what awaited me. I arose from the consoling calm of the cloud and glanced around me.

To my left was a silver pathway that seemed as if it were grayed out like a part of a computer program that was temporarily unavailable. To my right was an enormous building of exquisite beauty. A twenty-foot tall angel stood before me. His hands pointed in the direction of the building and I knew which way I was supposed to go.

I nodded my head in obedience and an instant later I found myself just inside doublewide white French antique doors. Sparkling diamonds were inset into the doors in a pattern that reminded me of a star chart. A very bright pure white light shone behind me and an enormous circular room stood before me. The diamonds in the door twinkled and sent a thousand prismatic beams of light glimmering around the room. I stood in awe, momentarily confused and afraid. A beam of soft blue light appeared and moved through me. A soft simple melody began to play from an unseen source and I began to again be at ease and relaxed.

Directly in front of me was a beautiful wall of bookshelves in the cleanest and most brilliant color of white. The bookshelves were made from a material that seemed both solid and translucent and they were lined with silver and gold edges. They glimmered and the reflected light of the diamonds in the door danced over the bookshelves and books and created a tranquil and beautiful scene. There was no apparent pattern to the placement of the big heavy looking white hardbound books on the shelves. Some books stood alone and others stood in clusters of two, three or four. Each book was about thirty inches tall and seven inches thick. Large golden letters that were unfamiliar to me were imprinted on each books spine and the letters seemed to be sending a cryptic message just outside my ability to comprehend. I noticed that a number of books were on each shelf and maybe three-fourths of the bookshelves were full. I smiled and gave this place the name the Library on the Other Side.

To my left there was a gloriously ornate circular white brick fireplace. A fire of white and gold flames was burning brightly but there was no obvious fuel for the fire. Golden sparks and beams of silver shafts of light shot from the flames. Occasional green, blue, yellow and rose flames appeared and the effect was something like watching a thousand colored lights reflecting on a lovely water fountain. It was soothing to watch the fire burn; and I had the feeling that I could have stood there simply enjoying the fire for what I once referred to as years. Each brick of the fireplace was imprinted in gold with the same style of unfamiliar letters present on the book spines. Some bricks seemed to stand out toward me while others were pushed back and yet others were situated in between. One brick was glowing with a rose-colored light as if a separate fire were burning within it. I started to reach out and touch the brick, but a trumpet sounded and drew my attention away. It was such a pure sound that I was astonished at the splendor of its clarity. The sound seemed to come from my right and I turned in that direction.

The World Beyond: The Library on the Other Side

I saw a giant picture window that looked out over a green palm laden beachfront. White waves capped with gold froth rang with the most beautiful musical tones as the waves flowed toward green, white and gold colored rocks. Silver birds unlike any I was familiar with soared through a sky of gold and deep purple. It reminded me of a sunrise on the clearest of mornings in the most tropical of places and it seemed to bring peace and serenity to my soul.

My attention shifted back inside the room. The ceiling must have been a hundred feet tall and far above me I could see what appeared to be paintings of angels. Surrounding the angels were unusual animals and a field of emeralds growing in a garden of stunning mystical colors with which I was unfamiliar. The paintings were truly three-dimensional and I marveled at the talent of the artist. I wondered how he or she had accomplished this marvel. I smiled at the beauty of the art and I heard the cheerful ringing of distant bell. For a few moments the light in the room seemed to intensify. I looked around and was amazed at the glistening harmony of colors.

In the center of the room there were two things that were so unusual that I could hardly believe my eyes. A large three-dimensional silver symbol reminiscent of a music treble cleft sign was both centered on the plush white carpet, and inside the carpet. I did not understand how it could be so, but it was. On one side of the fireplace there was a series of several bowls that seemed to be lighted with music and glowing with a plethora of colors. Music seemed to bubble up from the bowls visibly as one might expect water to bubble from a fountain. I placed a hand over the bowls and the music began to change. I noticed that the bowls seemed to vary in temperature as well as in musical tone. Each movement of my hands produced an ever-changing musical masterpiece and I enjoyed the interactive symphony that I was creating. I learned how to change the melodies, the harmonies, the tempo and the rhythm.

A flash of light that reminded me of lightning striking garnered my attention. The flash seemed to come from the bookshelves and I looked in that direction and saw that one of the volumes had begun to twinkle. A sparkling five-point star of glimmering silver appeared on the book's spine and the entire book began to vibrate. Smooth soothing energetic and graceful musical melodies flowed from inside the book. I reached for the book and saw that my hand was now as Joan's hand had been when I had left my body. It was not the hand of a body at all, but a hand of pure energy. There was a vague shape of a hand encased in a glove of intense white light. I touched the book and caressed its cover. Instead of being like books I had picked up with my old body, this book was both soft to the touch and a source of a deep peace. I lifted the book and was surprised to find that it had no weight at all. The heavy vibration of the book subsided and now it seemed to purr gently in my hands. I turned from the bookshelves and a table and two matching chairs appeared from nowhere. The table was simple, round and radiantly white and each of the chairs appeared soft and comfortable. I sat down and placed the book on the table. I started to open the book, but my mind drifted back to how I had come to be here.

I remembered that I had died and the memory was only unpleasant because I was concerned if Lee and Sara were all right. I felt that I had to know if they were all right. I could not rest until I knew. I could progress no further. I stood, pushed back the chair and walked back through the open doors and out of the Library.

Paul L. Bailey

Chapter 4

Everything changed. A large sheet of liquid light leapt towards me. Its focus adjusted first into a brilliant spotlight then it dissolved into a dreamy haze. The sheet of light swiveled and tilted and swayed and I found myself moving with it and through it. Or was it that the light was moving through me? I could feel the dense cold of winter and it chilled my soul. Then there came the sound of a thousand voices and a million distorted musical tones together in a dark dissonance and jolting jangle. I seemed to rise and falland drift and float in the sea of sounds and in the absolute glaring intensity of the light. It was so bright that I could not see and so loud that I could not hear. It was as if everything simultaneously shifted and within the shift there was an inky oily blackness and a subtle discontinuity.

I stepped forward thinking only of Lee and Sara and as suddenly as the great shift of things had begun it now ended. I found myself standing in a tiny viewing room in a funeral parlor. The lights here appeared muted and the colors around me looked washed out. There was something else that was not quite right either but I could not think what it was. At the front of the room, a rosewood casket was placed on a metal stand and numerous flower arrangements stood nearby. I looked toward the casket, but I could not see inside. Every time I looked in that direction, I saw only a vale of darkness.

Lee came into the room and stood looking into the casket. He was crying softly and I wished that I could tell him that I was right here behind him and not in that casket. I wished that I could share that the real me was not dead. I wished that I could tell him that there was no such thing as death to the soul. I remembered that Joan's spirit body had been able to move my broken body and then I remembered I had asked her to do that – demanded that she do it. I could not move Lee's body while he was still inside of it. Instead, I allowed myself to draw close to him and I simply placed my spirit arms around him. Lee immediately stopped crying and looked around wide-eyed. He could not have known it, but he was looking right at me when he whispered, "Leena?"

I allowed myself to pass through him and I saw Lee close his eyes in pleasure.

"Leena!" Lee whispered.

He stood there for a few minutes with his hands out in front of him as if he were in a darkened room and searching for the light. Tears formed in his eyes and I longed to wipe the tears away. He turned, looked back into the casket and he must have touched the body that had once been mine. He said aloud, "Good night, my love. I'll be with you soon," then he walked from the tiny room.

Things blurred and shifted again, as they had before, and I heard a gentle crying. The sound of the crying transported me to the bedroom of my daughter Sara. I knew that she was overcome with grief. I moved my spirit hands and touched Sara's forehead. I wanted her to sleep; and she fell into a peaceful slumber. I took Sara into a dream of a beautiful flower garden set in green rolling hills near the sea. In the dream I told her that I would always be here with her in her memory and that everything was going to be all right. When Sara awakened I knew that she would be fine.

Things shifted again and I found myself standing in the same cemetery where Seth was buried. The rosewood casket was closed now and covered in greenery and flowers. Many of the people I had known in my life as Leena stood around listening as Pastor Rick read a scripture. Macy Boyce sang a hauntingly beautiful but simple a cappella version of *Amazing Grace*. Lee seemed unable to speak and he simply stood holding Sara's left hand. A handsome young man that I had never met stood at Sara's side holding her right hand. My parents were there and standing to their left was a sober well-dressed Alan that I almost did not recognize. His toupee was gone and for the first time since childhood his face was without the flush of alcohol.

"Today we are here to honor the memory of Leena Ann Melvin Woods," Pastor began. "Leena was the beloved daughter of Roy and Lynn Melvin and the sister of Alan Melvin. She was the wife of Leland Thomas Woods and mother of Seth and Sara Woods. Seth is laid to rest in this cemetery and Mrs. Woods will be laid to rest beside him. Leena was born in Tillamook, Oregon and graduated from Astoria High School. She achieved her degree from Portland State University. Leena was involved in many church activities including Vacation Bible School and choir . . . " The pastor continued speaking but I lost interest in his words.

Again things blurred and shifted and I sensed that time had passed. I found myself in a large church decorated for a wedding. I stood and watched as Lee led Sara down a wide and beautifully decorated aisle. White orchids and white ribbons contrasted with the deep mahogany wood and the effect was a rich and beautiful wedding setting. The wedding march was in progress and when Sara and her father reached the front of the church, he gave her hand to Jon Sessions. Jon was the handsome man I had seen holding Sara's hand at my funeral. Now the couple looked a few years older, happy and in love. I watched the ceremony and then followed the guests into the reception hall.

"I just wish Mother could have been here," I heard Sara say.

"I believe she *is* here, in her own way," Lee said.

I smiled.

Lee looked much older. His hair was silver now, and he had gained twenty pounds. He walked with a slight limp. He moved through the reception with his walking cane and talked with everyone. He spoke briefly with Alan and shook his hand and he spent a few moments with Macy and her now teenage children. Danny now stood nearly six-foot tall. He was dressed in a nicely cut tuxedo and he looked both sweet and gorgeous. Marie, still tiny at only four-foot-eleven looked radiant and beautiful in her peach colored formal dress.

I saw that Joan was again by my side. She smiled and I knew that it was again time for me to go. Joan took my hand and, in an instant, I found myself standing before the white table at the Library on the Other Side.

Chapter 5

The large white book still lay twinkling on the beautiful round table. I directed my attention to the book and began to carefully examine it. On the spine of the book the single name, "Lucretia" was neatly printed in beautiful script in the most intense gold color and texture. The sparkling letters were easy for me to read now, although I recalled that at first the lettering had seemed unfamiliar. The books pages were very thick and made of an exotic translucent material. I opened the book to look at the title page but noticed that it contained no paper pages, no written words, no artwork and no photographs. Instead, each transparent page projected a three-dimensional moving image. One page began to vibrate and I touched it in amazement.

Suddenly, I was gazing through the bright eyes of five-year-old Lucretia Titus. She sat in her tiny wooden chair within her simple home surrounded by sparse handcrafted wooden furnishings apparently made from scraps of material. I heard her mother saying, "This is 'C' – say 'C'." Lucretia's mother was dressed in a simple full-length black dress and white apron from the early nineteenth century. She was a simple looking young woman in her mid twenties. She wore no makeup or jewelry. Her flowing black hair was neatly combed and her soft brown eyes were filled with love and patience. She looked tired as she leaned to match Lucretia's level.

Lucretia first looked at the handcrafted wooden object that had been expertly shaped into a small flat paddle with a round handle just the right size for her hand. Then her eyes focused on the single piece of tattered yellowed rag paper that had been affixed to the flat of the wooden paddle with some sort of rudimentary paste. Each letter of the alphabet was carefully written on the paper first in uppercase than in lowercase letters. A verse from the Bible was written below the letters.

The girl's mother was pointing at an uppercase letter 'C' and I felt the child's mind struggle with the idea that this symbol had a sound attached to it. Her mother said, "This is a letter, its name is 'C'. Lucretia's eyes, my eyes, our eyes lifted to Mama. I felt Lucretia begin to understand and heard an idea begin to form in her mind. Lucretia's father sometimes referred to people in their family using only the Titus family name. He would say things like, "A Titus never lies."

"It is like me," Lucretia thought. "I am a Titus and my name is Lucretia. This is a Letter and its name is C."

As suddenly as she had begun to understand, her concentration evaporated and I began to smell the mouthwatering fragrances of food. Lucretia's Grandmother was standing over a large black steaming kettle and stirring something. It was the smell of a delightful mixture of freshly picked home grown vegetables. I felt Lucretia begin to wiggle and Mama let her down and went to help Grandmother with the meal. I understood that Mother was overwhelmed with the complexity of the endless tasks she had before her. She had pumped the water from the well, chopped the wood for fuel in her fireplace oven, and then baked flat bread. She had trimmed the candles, taken clothing to the stream and scrubbed it using a wooden scrub board. She had worked the garden, helped Grandma begin the dinner process, prepared the horse, and run a few errands for her husband. She had done it all while caring for an ailing Grandfather and an energetic five-year old child. She stretched herself to be the teacher, the mother, the caretaker, the wife, the gardener and so much more. Grandma tried to help but her aging body kept her from accomplishing many of the most difficult tasks.

The door flew open and a tall handsome red-haired man and a skinny blond boy of about twelve years of age walked into the room. The smell of the food quickly faded into the background and a joy so pure that only a child could contain it erupted in Lucretia's heart. I could not remember ever feeling so much happiness.

"Papa," cried Lucretia.

Papa picked up Lucretia and gave her a kiss on the cheek. "Hello little Titus!" he said. When he put her down he handed her the handcrafted hornbook and turned his attention to his apprentice. Thomas Lee had joined the Titus family about a year ago when he had turned eleven. He was studying with Papa, Noah Titus to learn the cooper trade. Noah and Thomas began talking about something that Lucretia could not understand. The topic of their conversation concerned the trade Papa was teaching young Thomas.

Even though I was experiencing things through Lucretia's intellect and emotions, my own intellect was still at work. I understood that Papa was a cooper by trade and that a cooper was a skilled craftsman who worked with wood and fixed anything made from wood. I looked around the room and I noticed the detail in the furnishings and the love that must have gone into the creation of each piece. Coopers made barrels, tubs, and buckets to store threshed grain, flour, molasses and the like. Dry goods were stored in something called a slack barrel and wet goods were stored in kegs. Papa was explaining to Thomas how a certain type of barrel was made.

Lucretia lost interest in the conversation and turned her attention to the sound of the door opening.

Grandpa came into the house and the men folk were soon seated at a small table. Mama served the men first, including Mr. Lee. Papa always insisted that the women folk treat Mr. Lee as an adult and not as a child. That meant that everyone in the household referred to him formally and not by his Christian name.

Grandpa had recently been ill with the fever and he seldom worked with Noah and Thomas. Grandpa's skin had a horrible unnatural yellow color and his gray hair was falling out in clumps. He usually worked in the house with the women or alone at his own pace in the shop while Noah and Thomas took on the real work. Grandpa had made the hornbook that Lucretia was using to learn the alphabet and the quill pen Lucretia would later use to practice her writing. He made candles to help light the small house at evening. No one would say it, but everyone felt that he didn't have long to live. Grandpa remained optimistic and worked hard at his new tasks.

Mama brought Lucretia some food that she had earlier set aside to cool. Lucretia had been turning the hornbook first one way then another in her small hands. Now she set it aside and began to eat with enthusiasm. I began to think that every sense that Lucretia could experience was mine to experience also. I could see every sight that she saw, hear every sound that she heard, touch, smell and taste every thing just as she did.

The Earth began to shake and the wind began to howl. Lightning flashed and thunder roared. The tiny house began to tremble as if it were afraid. I felt Lucretia's eyes widen and I knew she must be afraid. Yet I felt no fear. I began to understand that I could not experience Lucretia's negative emotions. They were not accessible to me. I wondered why.

Lucretia grabbed the hornbook and held onto it with all her strength. Frigid rain fell in a torrent and hail formed. The sound of the hail fall echoed in the evening darkness. A moment later an icy gust of wind blew the door wide open and the straw sleeping mattress lifted from the floor and sailed into a quaking wall. The mattress seemed to twist itself into shreds and the remnants blew around the little home's single room. A small wooden container was wind swept from the table. It lifted and began to spin as it flew and hit Lucretia's arm. I heard her screaming as if I myself were screaming. Yet I felt no pain.

Papa shot from the table and rushed to the door and tried to hold it closed. The wind's blowing increased and the Earth's quaking intensified. Bolts of lightening scattered themselves across the darkened sky and thunder answered as if in reply. Cold rain fell and the strong wind blew the rain into the little house. The black kettle collided with Grandma and fell to the floor spilling its contents. Grandma fell too and the weight of the still nearly red-hot kettle rolled and settled on her fallen body. The winds angry howling cut off her screams of pain and then an eerie stillness fell as the wind went silent. Grandpa rushed to Grandma's side, but it was too late. He sat there on the floor with his arms around her body, his head buried in the charred strands of her white hair.

Time seemed to slow. The tears in Lucretia's eyes and the blood on her hands blurred my vision. Lucretia held stubbornly to her hornbook as if it were an anchor to life itself. She rubbed at her tired eyes with her free hand and left streaks of blood soaked hair across our field of vision. The wind abruptly ended its silence and with renewed vicious furry it sent the oil burning lamp that had been hanging in the center of the room to the floor. The lamp exploded on impact and the crackle of fire from the lamp licked at the bits of straw mattress, wooden furniture and the wooden walls. Fire seemed to burst from everywhere. The smell of acrid smoke started Lucretia and the others coughing and choking. I could see the smoke too, but it did not distress me. Thomas covered his mouth with his sleeve and went to help Papa. Together they tried to fight the fire, but Papa's clothing soon caught fire and he screamed and fell.

The sound of the rushing wind sang in chorus with the sounds of creaking and popping wood and the whooshing of the fire lapping at the walls. Unlike Lucretia, I experienced it all without any kind of fear, pain or discomfort. I discovered that although this all seemed very real, and indeed it was real, that I was only here as an observer. I could do or say nothing. It seemed that I 'was' Lucretia. My viewpoint was from what she could see. I could not see her face but I could see a portion of the handmade white cotton shirtdress that we wore and the bright red blood spots that stained it. I could see her - our little spindly legs and arms. I could see a wisp of red hair that was partially in our eyes and the small blood splattered hands that continually rubbed crying sleepy eyes.

I heard the icy sound of the wind again, felt the Earth's quaking begin anew, and saw that the roof of the house had begun to collapse. It was a strange sensation to see the smoke, understand that the house was burning and crumbling around me and yet feel no fear. It was stranger still to realize that a small child was in serious danger, and to know that in some sense I was that child and yet feel at ease with the fact that I could do nothing to help.

Mama scooped Lucretia up in her arms and fought through the burning doorway. I saw a fleeting glimpse of Mr. Lee as he jumped from the burning house behind Mama and then I felt the pressure of the wind's chill in contrast to the heat. Lucretia buried her head in her mother's clothing and I could see nothing more. The page before me became opaque and another page began to vibrate. I turned to the page and found myself again seeing through Lucretia's eyes.

Lucretia was now ten years old. Mama and Mr. Lee were the only people here with her that had been in the burning house. I knew that Papa, Grandpa and Grandma had died in the flames of yesteryear. A tall dark sinister looking man stood watching Lucretia. He was an older man and his name was Steven Pritchard, but Lucretia referred to him only as Sir. Sir was the master of this house and the new husband of Lucretia's mother. He was a rich man accustomed to having things his way. He was an unpleasant man with a fat bushy mustache and thick oily black hair. A twisted red scar stood raised a fraction of an inch below his left eye. His hands were soft and small and he smelled of tobacco and bay rum.

His house was much larger than the one that had burned. His house wore the markings of wealth while the one that burned had worn the markings of poverty. Here there was no simple single room of Earth floors and straw mattress. Here there was no single hanging black kettle or burning oil lamp. Here there was no hard labor from sunrise to sunset. Here there was luxury and plenty, but here too, there was a terrible secret.

Within Lucretia, where once lived the great joy of her father now lived only shame, sorrow and confusion. Hidden deep beneath her own bed was the seared remains of the handmade hornbook she had rescued from the fire. It was all she had left of her father and his love. I knew Lucretia's secret, for I shared the ability to look deep within her troubled spirit; and what I knew, I did not want to know. I saw the secret fester within Lucretia and turn her from the beautiful, loving, innocent child she had once been into a person forced into a life of adult treachery at far too tender an age. I watched her silent struggle to keep her tears at bay. I watched the pretend smile with which she tried to tell her mother that she was all right. Lucretia knew that as long as Mama lived with Sir that Mama would have the riches that Sir could provide. Even if the cost to Lucretia was so high, she could not bring herself to tell her mother the secret.

Over the years, between the time of the fire and the time of Sir, Lucretia and Mr. Lee had become great friends. He treated Lucretia as an equal and never spoke down to her. He asked Lucretia to call him Tom but Lucretia felt that Papa would not have wanted that much familiarity. She finally agreed to call him Thomas when she turned eight years old. Thomas loved Lucretia as he would have loved a younger sister. In his eyes, Lucretia was a beautiful and precious young lady. A young lady that should be honored and cared for – cherished and adored. Thomas had grown into a tall good looking light haired young man with a full beard and sparkling indigo blue eyes. He had used his budding skills as a cooper to support Lucretia and her mother until mother had met Sir.

I wished that I had not known Lucretia's secret – for to know it and not be able to feel sorrow seemed wrong. I knew that she would one day share the secret with Thomas. I had seen the idea already form in her mind and she was planning the right time and circumstances. The memory of the fire had made Thomas her closest friend and she would tell him even the darkest of secrets. One day, Lucretia would tell Thomas that Sir came into her bed in the still of the night. She would confide that Sir did terrible, mysterious and detestable things to her. I knew that on the day that Lucretia finally gave in and told Thomas the secret, that Thomas would kill Sir. It seemed that then the same wicked man would destroy not only one, but two children. To know this secret as well as the impending fate awaiting Thomas and to be unable to do anything at all to help seemed wrong.

A part of my soul cried out not in pain but in frustration. When my soul cried out, all the pages of the book became opaque and I was left sitting alone at the table. The room around me still held its beauty and the fire was still burning brightly. I turned and watched peacefully as the fire burned. I allowed my mind to rest and I allowed the peace that passes understanding to again take up residence in my soul.

Chapter 6

I sat staring at the book as it lay in my lap and noticed that it looked much less interesting and somehow smaller now that it had stopped twinkling. I looked up from the table and noticed that something else had changed. The diamond-studded doorway that had been filled with light when I entered the Library had closed at some point while I was viewing Lucretia's story. The door had not only closed, it was now no longer visible.

I sat the book back on the table and allowed myself to relax into the comfort of the chair. Soothing clear glorious music surrounded me and I rested. After a moment Joan appeared in the room. She did not walk into the room, she simply appeared. Her clothing looked slightly different to me. Instead of a robe of pure light she was dressed in a stunning full-length one-piece hooded tunic made of an unfamiliar material. The tunic was such a brilliant white that it shone around her. On her left sleeve was a three dimensional representation of an outstretched human hand. One look at the representation and I understood that it signified Joan's position or purpose here. Joan was a Spirit Guide, a being whose purpose is to continually outstretch a helping hand to everyone she serves. Standing next to Joan was a fair-haired young man in his middle thirties. He smiled at me with dazzling silver eyes and the very thought of being frustrated vanished. He was dressed in a tunic very similar to the one Joan wore except that on his left sleeve there was a three dimensional representation of a cupped human hand holding a ball of light. I looked at my own left sleeve and saw the same symbol. Somehow I understood that this man and I were both souls in transition.

"Hello Leena," said Joan. "I would like to introduce you to Noah."

Noah smiled at me again and lifted his left hand to waist level. He held his hand palm up and gently moved his hand upward an inch or two. The book on the table rose and slowly turned in a gentle circular motion. Beams of rainbow colored light shot from the book until the book was surrounded by color. The book seemed to turn more rapidly now. Faster and faster it spun. A small bright ball of pure white light emerged in the center of the colors. The ball of light grew and became brighter until the entire book was surrounded by light.

Beams of white light together with beams of pale green light filled the room and the body of a young woman dressed in colonial garb formed from within the light. She extended her arms, palm up to either side of her body and the light began to shift until she stood before us like an angel back lighted in white light. I stared in amazement at this woman and wondered if she were an Angel.

"No, Leena," came the voice of the woman. "I am not an Angel. My name is Lucretia. I am the spiritual embodiment of the person's life you were recently reviewing. I am here to answer your questions," she said.

"Lucretia?" I asked.

"Yes, Leena," she smiled.

I noticed that Joan had disappeared from the room as easily as she had appeared, but my attention was on Lucretia. The man that had been with Joan now stood silently watching me his arms lightly folded over his chest. I looked around the Library again and focused again on Lucretia.

"Lucretia, those were horrible things that happened to you! How you must hate that terrible Mr. Pritchard!" I said.

"Hate Steven? Why should I hate him?" Lucretia asked.

"He did terrible things to you. He hurt you as a child to satisfy his own depraved lust," I exclaimed.

"He did exactly as it was planned for him to do," Lucretia said calmly.

"Exactly as it was planned?" I asked incredulously. "You planned to be abused by some creep when you were ten years old?" I asked more loudly then I had intended.

"Yes, in a manner of speaking," Lucretia said.

I did not understand this at all. I was confused, or Lucretia was insane. How could what she is saying make sense? "Why on Earth would you plan such a thing?" I asked in puzzled amazement.

"Before I can answer your question I must familiarize you with one of the terms we use here. We refer to what you call your life on Earth as a Visit. A soul's true life is often much more than one Visit, so using the term *life* to refer to one Visit to Earth seems inappropriate to us here," Lucretia said.

I nodded impatiently.

"I think the question you intended to ask is why I would choose such a thing. The answer is that you are looking at a single piece of a gigantic puzzle and trying to judge the entire picture. You see only one thing Steven did in one Visit. What you do not see is the entire picture of Steven. During a different Visit, Steven was the doctor who risked his reputation, his career and his freedom to perform an untested medical procedure that saved my mother's life. I was three years old when Steven did that and in a manner of speaking he saved my life too. In another Visit, Steven was the father that took care of me, his hopelessly handicapped daughter. He gave up every pleasure, every moment in his life so that I might live another day, another hour. In yet another, Steven was the husband who rescued me from an abusive uncle. When the Planners suggested that Steven do a Visit where he was an abuser so that he could better understand the issue of abuse, he agreed. The Planners were looking for a volunteer to be the abused child, and since Steven had helped me so many times, I volunteered. It was my turn to help him," Lucretia answered.

I frowned, still confused and bewildered.

"The question you actually asked is why I would choose to do such a thing on Earth. The answer to that part of the question is easier. I have Visited Earth on several occasions as you can see by the filled volumes here in the Hall of Review or what you refer to as the Library on the Other Side. I chose to have this experience on Earth because Earth is one of the available so-called physical places where learning experiences can occur and because I prefer Earth to the other physical locations I have visited.

Here there is no pain, no suffering, and no long-term discomfort of any type. It's difficult to have experiences that one can learn from under those conditions." Lucretia said.

I was speechless and still baffled.

"Let me try to clear things up for you, Lucretia – uh, Leena," Noah started. "Things are not as they seem," he said. Then he settled into the chair opposite to me and began to speak openly. "When a soul first makes the transition from Earth to here, a place I call Home, the Planners try to make the transition as easy as possible. That is why you are observing this area in the three-dimensional model that you are accustomed to on Earth. Only one hint was left for you here as to the truth about dimensionality just as one hint was left for you in the garden. Do you remember?" Noah asked.

"You are talking about the fish in the pond and how some seemed to swimming above the pond," I said.

Noah nodded smiling

"Yes, and here you noticed the representation of a musical note that is both in and on the carpet. So, you should not be surprised if I tell you that there are more than three dimensions," he said.

"I have always thought that there might be a fourth dimension of the mind and a fifth dimension of the spirit," I commented.

"You have done well to consider this," Noah said. "But what if I were to tell you that there are more than five dimensions? More than fifty dimensions? More than five thousand? What if I told you that there are an infinite number of dimensions and that each dimension is as easily observed and worked with here as height, width and depth are observed and worked with on Earth?"

"I still don't understand. What does this have to do with Mr. Pritchard? Why wouldn't Lucretia still hate him after he abused her? And what are Planners?" I asked.

"I'm getting there," Noah said. "A group of beings known as Planners decided to create what I will call a 'wheel of time' on Earth. You might envision this construct as a disc or a sphere; I see it as a wheel. However you choose to see time, you can notice the circular aspect of it. Day follows night and then night follows day. The purpose of the circle is to establish a picture or type of the cyclical nature of things. The details are a bit complicated – so let me try to simplify it. Picture if you will a wagon wheel with eight spokes. At what speed does the wheel move?"

"That would depend on a number of factors including what is moving the wheel," I answered.

"Precisely, but humankind forgot to consider that fact when they began to try to measure time as if it were an absolute. For example, people measure the space between two of the spokes in the wheel, or two distinct events, and then refer to that measurement in terms of the tool they named time. If one spoke on the wheel or event in time is sunrise and the second spoke or event is the sun at the pinnacle – the period between the two could be named daytime. You can continue naming the space between the spokes or events on various time related wheels until you have arrived at days, weeks, months and years. What happens when a year ends? The New Year begins! The wheel has made a full circle. The problem is that no one considered what happens when someone or something changes the speed at which the wheel is moving. If the wheel moves faster, then time moves faster, if the wheel moves slower, then time moves more slowly," Noah said.

I started to object but Noah simply raised his hand and smiled at me again and I let him continue.

"It is from the basic idea of a *time of light* and a *time of darkness* that the concepts of *good and bad* as external forces or powers came into existence. Most of the religions and teachings on Earth consider the light *good* and personified by a *good* supreme being and the darkness *bad* or *evil* and personified by a *bad* or *evil* supreme being. I ask you; is it possible that good and bad are internal value systems that vary from person to person rather than external powers? Another way to ask is this question is to ask if *evil* is ever done during daylight hours or *good* done at night?" he asked.

"Of course," I said.

"Of course, indeed. You see these truths within the course of things, or within the wheel of things. Once people had settled on the belief that good and evil exist as external powers, their belief became active and they began to define or judge certain behaviors and attitudes as good or bad. The fact that good and bad are both simply judgments of some humans by others were lost – and good and evil were judged on how human behavior matched with various written and unwritten concepts. Do good and bad exist as external powers?" Noah asked.

"They must. Some people do horrible things to other people," I said.

"So you say, but what if I were to tell you that every action that ever happened to any person was planned and agreed to by the very person that the action happened to?" he asked.

"I would say that you are insane."

"So you say," Noah said still smiling. "Let us consider the implications if you are correct. Is it not true that some humans judge more harshly than others?"

I had to admit that some did.

"If good and bad exist as external powers rather than internal value systems, then why do some individuals choose to not honor the external power?" Noah asked.

"People have free will. They can follow which ever master they choose."

"Which of these people will decide which activities or actions are good and which are bad and who will decide the severity of the judgment for those actions judged bad?" Noah asked.

"Society can decide," I said.

"So you say. What is Society, if not simply a group of humans? Is society without fault?"

"No, but God can decide," I said.

"What if I were to tell you that God leaves judgment to humankind?" Noah asked.

"I thought God was the ultimate judge," I said.

"God is the ultimate everything. God chooses to allow others to judge," Noah said.

I considered this idea.

"It is when we understand that our view of good and bad is different from the view of others that we can begin to understand how important our internal value system is to us. People, at a societal level, set laws that the majority of people can agree are good or bad for the group as a whole. Yet, there are some people who see the majority's value systems as flawed and they work to undermine that system to bring attention to their own value system. This is a picture of what you may have called crime or terrorism."

"Isn't the will of the many greater than the will of the one?" I asked.

"The idea that most people agree absolutely on any one thing is unlikely to reflect reality. Each person has their own value system, created and nurtured by them and designed to allow the person to choose a perspective from within the reality they have created for themselves," Noah said.

"Are you saying that each person *creates* their own reality?" I asked.

"I am saying that each person can plan, create and approve the reality that they will face in their life or Visit," Noah said.

I narrowed my eyes and scrunched my face in response.

"What if I were to tell you that every soul is part creator, part master, part slave and fully everlasting?" asked Noah.

"I would say you truly are insane," I said.

Noah smiled patiently. "Imagine life as a type of time wheel. The spokes might include birth, childhood, youth, adulthood, old age and death. Now picture the Earth as a mother and as another type of time wheel. The spokes of this wheel might include Mother Earth conceiving from what is planted in springtime. In summer the plants begin to grow. In fall the harvest is taken and Mother Earth lays barren in the winter. Now think of a flower as another type of time wheel. The flower wheel exists within the Mother Earth wheel and the Mother Earth wheel exists within the life wheel. At the birth of the flower, the first green sprout is seen springing to life from the Earth. In the childhood of the flower, the bud of the flower forms. In the youth of the flower, its pedals begin to open. In the adulthood of the flower, the flower reaches its fullest potential, and in the old age of the flower, the pedals begin to lose their color and fall away. In death, the flower greenery has faded and its life has ended, only to return again the next season," Noah said.

I just looked at Noah. I understood what he was saying but I had no idea where he was going with it.

Noah smiled. "Each passing day can be seen as a wheel. The birth of a day is at sunrise when the sunlight breaks through to awaken the darkened sky. The childhood of the day is like the period between sunrise and midmorning. The youth of the day is between mid morning and noon and the adulthood of the day is between noon and sunset. Finally, the day fades and dies as the evening and night end – only to return anew the next day," Noah said.

"You are saying that everything dies and then lives again," I remarked.

"So you say. We indeed can see our lives or Visits to Earth as a type of wheel. We awake each day or are born to each day as the sun rises. We prepare ourselves for our day as we are prepared for our adult days in our childhood. We grow, attend school, and begin to work in our youth. In adulthood, we reach the apex of our career or personal development. We exchange the goods and services we can provide for the goods and services others can provide to us as we learn that we are all interconnected. The coming of evening is like the coming of old age. We may have time to relax and enjoy a portion of our 'day.' Then we grow tired and we lie down to sleep at night and that is like death. Do not forget that we also awaken again the next day to live again," Noah said.

I looked blankly at Noah. I still didn't understand what this all had to do with Mr. Pritchard.

"It is not for me to answer all of your questions, Lucretia. There will be others who will assist you along the way," Noah said.

"Why do you keep calling me Lucretia?" I asked.

"Have you not yet realized that you, Leena are also the being that was incarnate as Lucretia? Did you not notice the hints all around you? As Leena, your husband was Leland Thomas Wood. As Lucretia, your best friend was Thomas Lee. As Leena, your last name was Woods, as Lucretia both your father and Thomas Lee worked with wood. Do I need to continue or do you see?" Noah asked with a smile on his face.

"How can I be Lucretia and still see Lucretia standing over there?" I asked pointing.

"It is time for you to stop viewing yourself as if you were only capable of being in a single place and in a single time. That is a concept of Earth and now you are Home. The complete personality from each of your Visits is retained here so that you may benefit from their experiences and knowledge. You are free to communicate with these personalities in any way you choose." Noah said.

I understood and I was amazed that I had not guessed that Lucretia and I were one in the same before.

"There, Lucretia," said Noah, "that is the last question I am here to answer for you."

"What question?" I asked.

"The question of 'before.' You see, Lucretia, Leena, time was meant as a tool for Earth residents to use in measuring their life as well as a tool for the Planners to use to plan each life or Visit thoroughly – second by second. People have turned it completely around and allowed time to become a commodity, something to be traded and thus they have tied time with resources. Time was not meant by the Planners to become a resource," Noah said.

I let Noah's comments about time go. I had another question I wanted answered.

"You said something earlier about evil that I do not understand. Were you suggesting that we should ignore evil because it is planned for evil to exist?" I asked.

"You cannot ignore or acknowledge that which exists individually within each person as an internal value system, or as an ideal. Every being, every circumstance, and every event is created, planned or planted. Planning is not simply the act of thought; it is the action of implementing the thought. Just as simply thinking about planting a rose would do no good, just thinking about a plan has no effect. One must add action to thought and give up something of what they have to *plant the seed* so to speak. Then the plan can become or grow into reality. We can refer to all that is by using the simple word kernel, like a kernel of corn. Every kernel is planted by active planning before it grows by active purpose. When a kernel has grown, it is harvested by planned action and shared by common purpose. When a kernel transitions between wheels, Visits or lives, the kernel begins a review process or wheel. The purpose of the review process is not to judge or punish a soul. It is to help a soul learn from the education and experiences and to guide the choices that will be made in that soul's next phase of action or Visit. Once the soul has concluded its review, it makes choices and then it begins planning or planting to begin the creation of another reality or Visit, and on and on with wheel after wheel," Noah said.

"So, you are saying that good and evil do not exist?" I asked.

"No not at all. Good and evil do exist. They are the internal value systems of individuals and people use these systems to base their judgments upon themselves and other humans. If I ask you to help me learn a lesson that I can only learn by something you would conceive of as bad, or evil, would you be bad or evil to help me learn the lesson, or bad or evil to refuse me?" Noah asked.

"If I were your friend I might try to talk you out of doing something that might be harmful to you," I suggested.

"So you say. However, if you are a true friend and you understand that what ever happens on Earth can in no way harm that which is essentially me, then would you not be selfish to refuse to help?" Noah asked.

"Well, if you really wanted a bad experience, but why would you?" I asked.

"Why should you judge any experience desired by another soul as bad?" asked Noah.

I did not reply.

"If I limit my experiences to that which every being in existence would judge as *good* how many experiences would I have to choose among?" he asked.

"Well, I guess I see your point, but some people's actions are just evil. No one would want to experience that would they?" I asked.

"That is your judgment or internal value system speaking when you say that some actions are evil. In your most recent Visit to Earth did some people play games in which the character that represents them might do something that could be considered bad or evil? Didn't some people even play games in which they or others might die?" Noah asked.

"Well, yes, but that was only a game," I said.

"Why do you judge that experience a *game* and other experiences in your life *real*?" he asked.

"Because you can always turn a game off and go do something else. All you have to do is desire to end the game. If you are facing reality, you are stuck with the reality you are facing," I said.

"So you say, but what if I told you that you planned the very reality that you feel stuck in, and that you chose to feel stuck in that reality instead of choosing to feel free of it," Noah asked.

"On Earth sometimes you get controlled by your circumstances," I said.

"Not unless you choose to be controlled by them. You may choose to act as if you were controlled by circumstances or you may choose to act as if you control the circumstances, but no one or nothing is capable of controlling you against your will," he said.

"That is the first time that you disagreed with me. Before, you said, 'so you say' when I said something that you do not agree with, this time you simply disagreed," I said.

"It is not to agree or to disagree, it is to understand or not understand. When you made a comment that showed a lack of understanding I indeed have responded with "so you say." However, when you make a comment that you yourself know is not true, then it is not that you do not understand but that you have chosen to deceive yourself. This cannot be allowed, because deceiving yourself can be harmful, and here at Home, nothing that is harmful can be allowed," he said.

"All right, but I don't think you ever gave me a straight answer about why Lucretia shouldn't hate Steven Pritchard," I said.

"You are correct," Noah said, "I did not directly answer that question because Lucretia already answered your question and you chose to ignore her answer."

Lucretia spoke again as calmly as she had before, "Steven Pritchard did exactly as it was planned for him to do."

Noah smiled and spoke again more softly.

"Leena, it's really a simple concept to understand the idea of why a person would volunteer to go into a life or Visit that involved something that seems bad. Do you recall a television program from your youth called *Fantasy Island*?" he asked.

I nodded.

"People would go to the island and experience a fantasy for a week or two. It would not matter what fantasy they chose since it did not really affect their real life. After their week or two was over they would go back to where they live," Noah said.

I nodded again.

"Think of life on Earth as a week or two on a kind of *Fantasy Island*. What happens there does not matter at all in your real life. When it is over, you come Home," he said.

I understood what he was saying but life sure seemed like a lot more than a week or two in some fantasyland. Some of the things that had happened in my life sure didn't seem like a fantasy I would intentionally choose. I decided to change the subject. "Why was I on Earth in the first place?" I asked.

"Each soul has a purpose wheel to fulfill within their Visits to places like Earth. Each soul plans and chooses their purpose wheel and all the important elements of each Visit. Souls do all of this work here at Home before beginning their next Task or Visit," Noah said.

"What was my purpose?" I asked.

"If you do not know then you did not fulfill your purpose wheel." Noah said.

That stopped me for a minute and made me think. "So, are you telling me that all of these books are lives I have lived on Earth?" I asked motioning to the library in front of me.

"They are Visits that you have had to Earth and other such places," Noah answered. "They are also the outlines of potential Visits that you could choose to have," he finished.

"They are my future?" I asked.

Noah smiled warmly. "There you go again, thinking of things in terms of past, present and future, when you should now sense that everything is happening simultaneously. While you are experiencing me standing here speaking with you, others are experiencing me speaking with them, or working with them, or learning with them. There are thousands of things happening all at the same time."

"Talk about multi-tasking!" I exclaimed.

"Talk about it, indeed."

"What happens if the bookshelves get full?"

"There is no full," Noah said.

Noah placed his hands together in front of him at arms length. Then he raised each hand and moved each slowly away from the other. The walls of the Library began to vibrate and they all shifted. I saw that the circle had expanded and now there was an entire new bookshelf to the left and to the right of the bookshelf in the center. The bookshelves to the left and right were empty, then everything shifted again and the books were spread out in no apparent pattern across the entire width of the bookshelves. The number of books had not changed, but there was more empty space between the books.

Noah smiled, winked and started to disappear.

"Wait," I said. "Lucretia said that you were her father in her incarnation. That means that you were my father in at least one incarnation."

"Yes," Noah said with a warming smile. "Welcome Home, Little Titus."

Lucretia turned to me and spoke. Noah seemed to fade momentarily into the background.

"Almost every instant of your latest Visit contained conveniences that you took for granted. During my Visit, there was no electric alarm clock with a snooze button. There was no easy to set hot water shower you could simply turn on and enjoy. There was no store bought pre-sized ready-to-wear clothes to purchase from a retailer's shelf. All of these things you and many other people of your circumstance circle accepted as common. These *common* things did not exist during my time. I am not suggesting that my Visit was somehow more challenging than your own. I am simply saying that we choose the circumstance circle, or time period that best suits the purpose wheel we choose for our Visit. The circumstance circle is in constant inexorable motion and each tiny movement of the circle changes the circumstances that apply to Visitors in that period and after that period. It is not the shift from the light of day to the darkness of night that creates the sensation of time passing. It is the subtle synchronized shifts of the circumstance circle," she said.

I gulped. She continued to speak.

"You may wonder why I tell you these things. It is not to brag or judge or even to inform. My purpose is to give you hope and within that hope to add to your true life. No matter what the circumstances that circle a person's time on Earth, they exist as part of a grand plan that you have only lost track of for the briefest of moments. You do not need to be concerned with the circumstances that trouble you on Earth. A loving, caring, being placed those very circumstances before you with only your best in mind. It is easy to be on Earth and fail to see the beauty of a difficult circumstance, but that does not mean that the beauty is not there. Allow your sorrow concerning the circumstance to do its duty. Allow it to wash you clean of the action or lack of action that brought you to this circumstance and allow yourself to move foreword. This is my gift to you, Leena and to those who choose to share the secrets of your Visits. You are loved. <u>You</u> are loved," Lucretia said.

I stood enthralled by the love that sent these concepts from her heart to my own and saw within the truth of that love the fact that she and I were one.

"Why couldn't I sense your pain and your fear while I was viewing your life?" I asked.

"Home is a place where pain and fear do not belong. You were able to experience everything that is important to you without the pain and fear," she said.

Noah stepped forward and lifted his left hands. Lucretia's body shrunk from its full size to the height of the book, and she stood on the shelf just where the twinkling book had been.

"Things are not as they seem," cautioned Noah, and then he disappeared.

Paul L. Bailey

Chapter 7

Something in the room changed again and a door appeared where a window had previously been. Joan was in the Library with me and she motioned for me to rise from my chair. "Leena, by now you understand that more than one thing at a time can happen here. I would like you to use that ability now by coming with me while you continue to stay here and review your other past incarnations or Visits," Joan said.

I looked up at Joan wondering how I could accomplish this impossible task. Joan raised her hands in the same way that Noah had. Each of the books in the Library began to vibrate and shine. An explosion of a million different gleaming colored beams of light came from the books and when the light had faded I noticed that instead of books an army of book sized people were standing on the bookshelves.

"These are representations of all the bodies in which you once incarnated. One easy way for you to think about being in several places simultaneously is to imagine that you are leaving some of these people here to continue to review your past incarnations and you and some of the others come with me," Joan said.

"All right," I said. "That seems like it would be simple enough."

"Whenever you need an additional you, simply remember all of these," Joan motioned to the Library of many nodding and smiling people. At your call, each will acquire full size and come and meet us wherever we are so that you can both continue along the path with me and simultaneously explore the various places you find of interest along the way. To keep things simple, you may refer to any of these as Lucretia or you may refer to them as yourself," Joan said.

I asked a few Lucretia's to stay in the Library to review our past incarnations and walked outside into the bright light with Joan. The first thing I noticed is that there was no apparent source for the bright light – it was simply everywhere. There were no shadows, no shade and no cold or hot places. The light was beautiful and soothing. Its brightness no longer hindered my seeing clearly. The temperature seemed like a comfortable summer day on Earth and I began to think of this place as being like visiting Hawaii. As soon as the idea was in my mind, I noticed a change in my surroundings. There were palm trees, beaches and sand all within an easy walk. There were sunbathers, and cute little grass shacks scattered here and there. Hawaiian music played and young girls dressed in hula dresses swayed with the music.

"Wow! How did this turn into Hawaii?" I asked.

"You may choose to visualize your surroundings here to match any mood or preconceived idea," Joan said.

I turned my thoughts to the ski resorts of Aspen Colorado. I saw the granite crags of Independence Pass and then looked again and saw the Elk Mountain Range's spectacular fourteen thousand foot peaks. I saw skiers swoosh and lean and play in the drifting snow and majestic mountain air.

I could hardly believe it. "It works!" I said.

"Yes, and although anyone else can choose to be in the same surroundings you are in, they can also stand right next to you in completely different surroundings of their own choosing," Joan said.

We walked a little further and Joan spoke again.

"For now, I would like you to allow me to choose the surroundings so that I can give you a sort of tour of this portion of the Other Side," she said.

I focused my attention on Joan, and at once I saw a very unique building. The building was huge and in the shape of an octagon within an octagon. Each section of the octagon had eight individual sides, but instead of each side being straight, each had a complete circle within it, above it, below it, around it, and through it so that it was as if the building was overlapping itself. It looked like many buildings built on the same exact location and yet all in the same building.

"Each of the circles is someone's personal Library of Visits and potential possibilities," Joan said.

Even as Joan spoke, the others I had left within the Library began to share the stories and events of my various previous Visits and to write themselves upon my memory. I was in China or Austria, Germany or Africa, Japan or Mexico. I was poor or wealthy, healthy or sick, popular or alone. I lived in the thirteen hundreds or the seventeen hundreds, in the sixteen hundreds or in the time before Christ. I had what I considered good times and what I considered bad times and each time, when my task or purpose wheel was completed or when I bypassed my task or purpose because of my choices on Earth, I returned to the Library.

"You are looking at a representation of about two-million circles. In reality, there are enough circles so that every soul that has or will ever Visit may have his or her own Library. You may feel free to leave Lucretia here to learn from anyone's previous Visits or Purpose Tasks. Someone else will explain the concept of Purpose Tasking a little later," Joan said.

I decided to leave Lucretia here at the Hall of Review to study as many of these lives as possible while Joan and I were continuing along our tour.

"Leena, are you certain you want Lucretia to study as many lives as possible?" Joan asked.

Then I realized that there truly was no such thing as time here at Home. If I asked Lucretia to study as many as possible, I was asking her to review every life of every soul that had ever been on Earth. I decided to ask Lucretia to review the Visits of one hundred souls instead. "You keep answering my thoughts before I speak them," I said.

"You can do it too. In fact, you *are* doing it. You have not spoken one word aloud since you walked back into the Library after your visit back to Lee and Sara. Here, we communicate by thought. As in most things here, you may choose to experience other beings thoughts as sound, pictures, or any other way you choose to experience them," Joan said.

I started to ask another question, it seemed I had so many, but I noticed a beautiful blond haired young girl playing with a golden retriever on a lovely grassy knoll a couple of hundred yards away. The big dog looked similar to my dog Wally. As soon as the thought had come to me, I was where the girl and the dog were playing. "How did I do that?" I asked Joan.

"We travel here by thought as well. Do you remember when you had your out of body experience in the hospital during your incarnation as Leena?" She asked.

"Yes, I noticed that when I wanted to be near Lee, I was suddenly right next to him. I couldn't figure out how to relate to him since I was out of body," I said.

"There is a way for those out of body to relate to those in the physical body – but it's a little advanced for you while you are primarily at the Hall of Review," Joan said.

I decided to let the question go. If Joan considered the topic advanced, I was certain that I would have difficulty understanding the answer. I took up another question. "When I returned to see Lee after I left Earth, why couldn't I see into my casket?" I asked.

"Do you remember when you were floating above your body before you left Earth?" Joan asked.

I acknowledged that I did remember.

"As long as you could see your body you could go back into your body. As you recall, you did go back into your body just before you left Earth. On your visit to the funeral parlor, if you had been able to see your body, you could have reentered it. That could have caused a number of unintended and unplanned circumstances," Joan said.

"Newsflash: embalmed lady is raised from the dead?" I asked.

Joan smiled a yes.

"When I was at the funeral parlor I noticed that something else seemed wrong there but I could not figure out what it was. Can you help?" I asked.

"What you noticed that seemed inconsistent was that not all of you was there in the funeral parlor. A portion of you, or if you prefer; another you was still here at Home. It is similar to what you are doing now. A part of you is with me and other parts of you are accomplishing other tasks," Joan said.

I smiled and nodded. So that was it, I literally wasn't all there. "Is that the reason my trip back seemed so bumpy?" I asked.

"No. The reason your journey seemed so rough is that you went about it in a manner other than that was planned. When you set upon a path that has not been planned either by you or the Planners, things can get a bit bumpy," Joan said.

"When I was in the Library I heard a distant bell. Where did it come from?" I asked.

"It came from within you," Joan said.

I looked up at Joan astonished. "From within me?" I asked.

"Certainly. Your soul is awakening and it recognized the power of a smile and rang a bell to celebrate you finding one," Joan said.

Joan and I were suddenly standing in a place that was quite different from where we had been. We were standing in the only darkened area that I had seen since I came Home. It reminded me of twilight on a peaceful country morning and yet there was a very subtle and intriguing difference. It was neither twilight nor daylight and yet it was somehow both. I found myself standing on what appeared to be a sea of glass. Below me lights were visible as if they were the lights of a busy city. Looking down at them vaguely reminded me of seeing the lights of a familiar city as an airliner reached the airport.

Joan spoke and I almost jumped in my total concentration on this sight. "This is the City of Glass," she said.

I nodded.

"It was not necessary for you to go out the Library door and return to Earth in spirit form to view your family. All you would have needed to do is come here. You may view any one you choose at any time and when they send messages to you in the way of memories or thoughts or even an "I wish" with your name associated with it you can retrieve those messages here," Joan said.

A moment later a little dark brown bear with shiny chocolate colored eyes walked toward me. The bear was dressed as a postal carrier and he stopped in front of me and began digging into his orange mailbag. He twitched his button nose and wrinkled his white eyebrows and handed me several bundles of what looked like mail. The bear chattered at me that I could not understand and then after a moment turned to Joan in frustration. Joan said something back to the bear in a language I had never heard before and the bear turned his back and walked away wagging his head as if amazed anyone that did not speak his language could possibly exist.

I turned and a completely clear table rose from the sea of glass below me. I sat my packages of 'mail' on the table and looked down through the glass. I saw an elderly Lee sitting on a tan colored lawn swing in the backyard of what must have been an apartment complex. Lee sat there, newspaper folded neatly on his lap, staring out into the pale blue morning sky. He wrapped a light blue jacket around him and sat forward to watch a busy squirrel. The squirrel, a typical brown bushy tailed creature, was standing on his back legs and holding a nut between his front paws and nibbling on the nut. Lee straightened himself and the sudden movement caught the attention of the squirrel. It seemed to freeze in place for an instant and then it dropped the nut and ran up into a nearby tree and out of sight. Lee sat back and looked at the newspaper in his lap. He patted the folded newspaper as if promising to read it later and sat back and looked up into the white dotted sapphire sky.

I looked in a different direction and watched a middle-aged Sara welcome a graying Jon Sessions back from work. I noticed photographs on the walls. Two large portraits hung side by each in easy view from anywhere in the front room. One portrait was of a handsome young twenty-year old boy named Tom. Somehow I knew he was Sara and Jon's oldest son. The other portrait was of a stunningly beautiful high-school aged girl of seventeen named Tara. Tara was Sara's pride and joy and that Tom was the apple of Jon's eye.

I turned again and the scenes below me seemed to fade into the distance. I picked up my 'mail' from the table and the moment I touched it all the messages swept through me like a wave. It was instantaneous and exhilarating. In that single second, it was as if I had time to fully read each message several times if I chose to do so and to sort them and file them as I felt appropriate. There were hundreds of messages from Lee. There were many that simply whispered, "I love you, Leena." or "I miss you." Others were longer messages Lee had spoken when visiting my grave. On those occasions, he spoke in the same manner we had spoken together in our marriage and it was both touching and romantic to feel his true lifelong love. There was one message from Seth that had apparently been sent in the seconds before he left Earth. It simply said, "Oh God, Mom, I messed up. I'm sorry." There were a few messages from Sara, my favorite of which was one she had sent when she was only nine years old, long before I had died. The message said; "Mom, I pretended to do my chores but I didn't really do them very well. I love you Mom." The message made me smile and I suddenly understood why I had given the children chores to do in the first place. It was not to relieve myself of work, it often took more work to correct the things the children failed to do that than it would have taken to just do the chores myself in the first place. The reason I gave them chores is so that they could learn how to do the things they would need to know how to do in their adult years. Lee had always suggested that the purpose of the chores was to teach the children how to take responsibility for something. From his viewpoint he was of course correct. To say otherwise would be to suggest that I had a better grasp of Lee's reality than he himself had.

There were a surprising number of messages from Alan. Most of these were messages thanking me for helping him find himself. I was glad to have helped, even if I had no idea what I had done that helped or how I had done it.

"As you have seen, the City of Glass allows you to visit or see loved ones whenever you desire. There are souls on Earth with the ability to share your thoughts with those who are still living. Earth residents call these people Mediums because they can seemingly move between the living and the departed. The truth is these people simply have been given access to the City of Glass and understand how to reach souls who are in the city," Joan said.

"You mentioned that my visit was bumpy because I did something in a manner other than that was planned?" I asked.

"Many Souls come here to the City of Glass to view their funerals or memorial services, visit their family members in dreams and even cause certain events to occur to let their loved ones know they are watching. When you left the Hall of Review and elected to go back to Earth you did so by making a decision that limited yourself. You chose to believe that you could not continue until you resolved your need to know what was happening on Earth. As a free soul you are unlimited in your potential so you were able to accomplish what you wanted, but when you fail to plan or at least allow the Planners to plan, the consequences are a journey more difficult than it needs to be," Joan said.

Chapter 8

Joan smiled and things around us changed. Now we were in an open grassy field with gently rolling hills. The scene around us went on for as far as the eye could see. "I would like you to learn about the true nature of things, are you willing to do that?" Joan asked.

I smiled and nodded.

Joan pointed into the open field and a huge clock tower appeared. "Consider this clock," she said. "This is what in your last Visit you would have called an old fashioned clock. Most of these clocks were round like the one before you. Do you remember how the insides of the clock were filled with many different sized gears and cogs?" Joan asked.

I nodded and immediately Joan and I were inside of the giant clock tower. We stood just behind its huge face and watched hundreds of wheels and gears whirring and clicking and working together. Joan pointed towards the gears and said, "None of the wheels or cogs would have a purpose if each did not assist other wheels and be simultaneously assisted by other wheels and cogs within the clock."

I nodded looking around at the huge gears and the complex and almost unfathomable way that they worked together.

"Imagine that each wheel and cog has a personality and a purpose," Joan said. As soon as she had spoken the words each wheel took on the appearance of an animated character. Each was still a gear but they each had a face and their personalities shone through the various faces. "It would be impractical for one part of the clock to hate, envy or judge another part – because after all, each is a part of the same creation – the same 'clock.' It is the same with mankind," Joan said.

I nodded, raised my eyebrows and tightened my lips.

"Now imagine that Earth is like a giant old fashioned clock," Joan said.

Joan and I walked into an Earth sized old-fashioned clock and saw individual clocks of various continents inside. Each continent clock contained the individual clocks of countries and inside the country clocks were the individual clocks of cities, towns and rural areas. Within these clocks were the clocks of neighborhoods and within these clocks were the clocks of individual families, and finally, within these clocks were the individual clocks of each person. All of these clocks were made up of many individual wheels. Each wheel had a name and a specific function or purpose.

"When we move the focus off each individual wheel or person and onto one of the larger clocks we see that everyone and everything is interrelated, all formed to accomplish a task and to simultaneously provide service to others just as we are provided service by many others. This is a picture of all of humankind," Joan said.

"Are you saying that people that do bad things are like a wheel within a giant clock and that what they do somehow fits the overall purpose of their wheel?" I asked.

"This is one way to understand it. Do not forget, however, that the clock must have a power source before the wheels can begin to move. Yet, even the concept of a power source is a like a wheel. Imagine that instead of the clock having only two hands, that the clock we are discussing has hundreds of billions of hands. Imagine that billions of these clocks are interconnected with more clocks and that on each complete cycle of each clock millions of more clocks come into existence. Each wheel within each clock is working together individually and collectively with each other wheel, all powered by the same Source," Joan said.

I smiled at the huge image Joan was describing as a view of it developed before me. I clamped my hands over my ears as I imagined the synchronized clanging of chimes from millions of clocks.

"During your latest Visit, you had the opportunity to see a modernized version of an invention by George W. Ferris called the Ferris wheel. It was one of the highlights of the Earth year 1893 Chicago fair and its many variations have graced many a fair since. Mr. Ferris created the wheel as an answer to Paris' Eiffel Tower. The original wheel had thirty-six wooden cars that could each hold sixty people. Imagine life as a type of Ferris wheel," Joan said.

We were outside of the clock tower again and now it transformed into a double Ferris wheel. Instead of the wheels rotating around each other, one wheel intersected with the other at a kind of transfer station. "Just as the car of a Ferris wheel serves as a vehicle to transport a person around the wheel, the human body serves as a means of transporting the Soul during our Visit," Joan said.

I watched as a character that looked like a cartoon ghost boarded the first Ferris wheel and it moved in a full circle and came to the intersection with a second wheel. The cartoon ghost exited the first wheel and stepped onto the platform of the transfer station. It moved around a small-unmarked area of the transfer station and then boarded a second wheel. Now another Ferris wheel above the second came into view.

"The soul may select a different vehicle on the second wheel and travel to the point where that wheel intersects with a third wheel. The soul may continue moving between wheels through many phases of the 'clock' type construct or Ferris wheel construct," Joan said.

"Why does the soul keep moving from wheel to wheel?" I asked pointing at the cartoon character ghost that seemed to move faster and faster from wheel to transfer station and then to yet another wheel.

"The objective is not to get to a specific place on any given wheel, but rather to enjoy the ride. Along the way we gain experiences and knowledge. Each time a Soul reaches a transfer station, it can apply the experiences and knowledge it has gained to its individual development and the collective development of others. This is a picture of the concept of infinity and a more accurate picture of life," Joan said.

"I think I get what you are saying. But, what is the purpose of the transfer station? Why not just go directly from death back to life?" I asked.

"It is tempting to want to see ourselves immediately going from what you referred to as *death* back to *life*. But, since we do not really lose our true life in what you call death, the picture is incomplete. We do not go from *death* to *life;* we go from *life* on Earth back to *life* in the World Beyond. Our transition is not truly between life and death but between wheels. Does summer end and then immediately begin as summer again?" Joan asked.

"Of course not," I said.

"When summer ends, fall is born. When fall ends, winter is born and when winter ends, spring is born. The Planners have placed clues all around you to the truth of things. When a Visit on Earth ends, life at Home may begin in the Hall of Review, which you have so well named the Library on the Other Side. When the purpose of the Hall of Review has been accomplished, Home life may shift to the City of Choices. When the purpose of the City of Choices has been accomplished, Home life may shift to the City of Planning. And then, when all of these purposes have been completed the next phase of your next Visit may begin," Joan said.

"You said that life on *may* shift from one city to the next. What do you mean?" I asked.

"There are many paths in the World Beyond, just as there are many paths on Earth. You have selected this path for this journey," Joan said smiling.

I sat stunned. The Hall of Review? The City of Choices? The City of Planning or Planting? What was she talking about?

"Be patient," Joan said. Then she extended her hand and things changed again.

Once again Joan and I stood on the lovely grassy knoll where the young girl and her dog were playing. I focused my attention on them and the dog came running over to me and began to lick my hands. He was waging his tail happily. The girl came over to me to and gave me a big hug.

"Hello," she said. "Welcome Home."

She was dressed in a beautiful pink and white party dress with white stockings and white shoes. She wore her long white blond hair in a braided ponytail. At first I was not certain that I knew this girl and then something about her changed and I saw her not as a young girl of twelve or thirteen, but instead as an elderly grandmother. As the way I saw the girl changed, the clothing that she wore changed. Now she seemed to wear a nice pink sweater, white skirt and white low heal shoes. Then it hit me. This was my great grandmother, Doreen Hanes! Great Grandma Hanes had helped my mother with me when I was a baby. I remembered being told that my mother had been very ill right after I was born and Great Grandma had left Jennings, Kansas to take care of Father and me while Mother regained her strength. I remembered that Great Grandmother Hanes's funeral had been the first one I ever attended. I had been ten years old.

I turned my attention to the happily panting dog. The dog seemed to know me and now I recognized him. It was

Wally! The golden retriever that Lee and I had owned. I wondered how he had come to be here so quickly.

"Wally lived twenty-one years in Earth time, Leena," Grandma said.

I was stunned. That meant that I had been here over fifteen Earth years. It seemed like less than a day since I had arrived. It did not matter. I shrugged off the time comparison and petted Wally. He and Grandma came with us as we moved along.

"Grandma, can you answer some questions for me?" I asked.

Grandma nodded. It seemed a family trait to nod instead of answer.

"On Earth, many people report seeing a tunnel with a bright light at the end and they still return to life on Earth. How can that be?" I asked.

"There is a place and a purpose for what Earth Visitors call Near Death Experiences. Just as is it true that a soul may choose how they desire to experience the World Beyond, it is also true that a soul can experience a Near Death Experience in any way they choose. Many choose to encounter the same primary experiences but there are many variations. The only limitation is that those who will return to Earth seldom actually get all the way to the Hall of Review," Grandma said.

"Where do they usually go?" I asked.

"They usually visit some variation of the garden that you first encountered," Grandma said.

I smiled and remembered that even when I took Sara into a dream after I had left Earth that I had even taken her to a variation of the garden. "On Earth, why are some people so much more materialistic than others?" I asked.

"Like most things on Earth, it is a matter of perspective. Some people on Earth believe that the life they are currently living is the one and only opportunity they will ever have to experience life in any form. They fear that when they die they will lose their ability to express love to themselves and to others around them and their knowledge of their mortality exacerbates their fear. To the degree that a soul believes that there is not enough of life, or enough of the things that matter most in life, that the soul's struggle will manifest selfishness, greed, discontentment and fear," Grandma said.

"So, some people are afraid they will lose what is most important to them?" I asked.

"Some are. They fear that since they have no memory of life before birth, that life must end at death. Some fear that after their current life is over there is only nothingness. Others fear that after their current life is over they will somehow lose their identity or individuality and become an insignificant part of some great cosmic consciousness, force or universe. Some people fear that they will fail to meet some greater being's expectations or criteria and therefore be destined to live out eternity in limbo or worse yet live out eternity in the fires of hell," Grandma said.

"Is there a limbo or a hell?" I asked.

"Anything you choose to perceive is available to you here," Grandma said.

"Are we in heaven?" I asked.

"Some call it heaven, some call it Eden or paradise, and some call it the World Beyond or the Other Side," Grandma answered smiling.

"What about heaven and hell?" I asked.

"In my opinion, heaven and hell are ideas or states of mind. If a soul chooses to see their surroundings here as heaven, they may do so. If a soul chooses to experience their surroundings here as hell, they may do that as well. It is just as you were playing earlier and experienced your surroundings first in Hawaii, then in Aspen Colorado," Grandma said.

"I was actually in neither Honolulu nor Aspen. I was simply experiencing those surroundings?" I asked.

"Yes," Grandma said.

"Cool, a direct answer! And you didn't say, so you say," I said.

Grandma, Joan and I laughed, and it seemed to me that Wally was laughing too. From above I heard the familiar voice of Noah.

"I heard that," Noah said, and there was laughter in his voice too.

"So, is the idea of heaven and hell a myth?" I asked.

"No, it is not a myth, it is a belief system. Every person is free to have any belief system they choose. Each soul chooses a belief system that best suits their design. The system each soul chooses fits that soul exactly right. May I share an idea with you of how I believe?" Grandma asked.

I nodded.

"Consider this. What if everything on Earth was created, planned, or planted by a power or source with no desire to harm any of us? Give this power or source any name you choose. Some call it God or Goddess, others call it Allah and still others have many other names by which they refer to the same source. The name one calls this power or source is not important. By whatever name, it is the source of all that exists. For the purposes of our discussion, let's agree to simply refer to this power as the Source," Grandma said.

I agreed.

"What if the Source has no need to judge us, criticize us, reward us, or punish us? What if the Source has no need or desire to control us or to shape us into any particular mold? What if molding us into something is exactly the opposite of what Source wants? What if what Source wants is for us to mold ourselves into what we have been created to become? What if the process of that molding is the very reason for life on Earth and other such planets?" Grandma asked.

"That's a lot of what ifs," I commented.

"Will you agree that it is a possibility that what I have described is one way to view truth?" Grandma asked.

I nodded.

"I believe that each of us is an eternal spirit being who has planned and volunteered for every aspect and condition of every Visit we have ever experienced or ever will experience. I think each of us made our choices to learn and grow individually and collectively as well as to help others grow individually and collectively. I think that along with all of that, we can choose to help others grow by incarnating as an individual, as an element, or as a Purpose Task," Grandma said.

"Are you saying we are part of some master plan?" I asked.

"Not only are we a part of a master plan, but we are also a master co-planner," Grandma said.

"Why would anyone willingly choose to have bad experiences?" I asked.

"I believe that we come to Earth to accomplish a set of purposes that some refer to as a purpose wheel. Our chosen purpose is not necessarily easy, but if we want to grow and learn, the purpose wheel is critical to our success. Sometimes the best way to learn an important lesson is to experience certain things that seem *bad* and to learn from those experiences. Eventually, when the experience is far behind us we can usually see the *good* that came out of the experience," Grandma paused.

We stopped near a large tree. The tree was so tall I could barely see the top. When I looked straight up I could see the giant leaves and branches reaching out toward the light. The trees roots were huge and partially exposed and the deep brown of the trees bark seemed to shine. A park bench appeared from nowhere and we sat down. Joan appeared and sat on a swing that appeared from nowhere. Wally sat directly in front of me and I ran my hands through his luxurious fur as Grandma continued.

"Within the ideas of good and bad are the experiences of pain and pleasure. As a part of our planning for a Visit we establish a control mechanism that defines the extent of our pain and pleasure experiences. It is important for us to experience both pain and pleasure because neither would be of value without the other as a counter point. Since we each establish our own parameters for pain and pleasure we cannot easily evaluate, judge or sympathize with the pain or pleasure of others. Others may experience a circumstance that seems to be exactly the same as one we experience but they may experience a completely different pain or pleasure simply because they chose a different pain and pleasure scale," Grandma said.

Wally positioned himself to take a nap and I noticed that the park bench became a comfortable overstuffed sofa. I sat back and relaxed.

"Since we are free to evaluate or judge anything about ourselves from our own viewpoint, pain and pleasure can be as radically different between two people as their belief system can be. I believe that pain and pleasure are designed to serve as modalities within a Visit to create a search for the ultimate rest. The ultimate rest is not an issue of either pain or pleasure but rather it is that which is directly center of the two. I see pain and pleasure as opposites of the same spectrum. Life's objective is not to remain within either the realm of pain or the realm of pleasure but to reach a center point and choose that center point as a life focus area. I believe our bodies serve as a type of vehicle that carries our spirit through a Visit; much in the same way an automobile serves as a vehicle to carry our bodies between various geographical regions when we are on Earth. While an automobile may be replaced if it malfunctions, our body must carry us all the days of our Visit. Because of this, it is important that we protect our vehicle or body so that we can get the most from our Visit. Our vehicle or body must obey certain physical laws that relate to it and within those physical laws is the universal law of pain and pleasure. I believe that this universal law exists for a purpose that is not only dedicated to the physical or Earthly body but also important to the spiritual being that manifested the physical body. Within the manifestation of our body and within a chosen pain and pleasure modality the center of rest exists. The idea of the center of rest is coming to the spiritual place where circumstances are less important than the learning of the lessons that we sent ourselves to Earth to learn. When our purpose wheel becomes our primary life focus on Earth, then whatever conditions or circumstances we are facing become obstacles between where we are and where we choose to be. Once we identify these obstacles, overcoming them is relatively easy," Grandma said.

A white rabbit walked up to us, sniffed at Wally and then casually walked a few feet away and began contentedly eating clover. Wally looked at the rabbit, twitched his ears, smiled and – well, laughed. I cocked my head and smiled at the strange sight.

"For a moment, we will pretend that good and bad exist as external powers. With that in mind, you may be able to recall some souls that tried to set up their Visits so that only the things they would consider good would happen to them. These souls may have been the talented movie stars that had all the money they could possibly need, or the sports superstars, the gifted artists, physicians, attorneys, the wealthy and the sons and daughters of these people. Tell me, Leena, did these people often have what you would have called the good life?" Grandma asked.

"Some did, at least for a while. Then it seemed like many of them got caught up in drugs, alcohol or bizarre personal behaviors," I said.

"In seeking to have everything be good, they ended up with nothing that was good. Since there was no *bad* to compare *good* with, the *good* things lost their significance. To understand and value the *good* in their lives, these people had to create something *bad*. Otherwise, nothing in their life would make much sense to them," Grandma said.

"I understand," I said.

"There is really more to it than that, because there are at least two sides to every experience. One could conceive of these two sides as good and bad, although I quite agree with Noah that good and bad are truly only judgments. When a soul chooses a *good* experience, a *bad* experience is on the reverse side. It is impossible to choose one without the other. Sometimes, a soul chooses what others would consider a *bad* experience to help another soul," Grandma said.

"I am still having trouble with why someone would intentionally choose bad things," I said.

"The idea of good is usually tied with pleasure and the idea of bad is usually tied to pain. One reason you may be having difficulty understanding why someone would choose something you judge as painful, is that you may not see the alternative," Grandma said.

I cocked my head.

"If good is pleasurable and bad is painful then it makes sense to choose good unless choosing pleasure now means the possibility of pain later. For example, if having a lot of money is good, why don't more people rob banks?" Grandma asked.

"They have a personal code of ethics that won't allow them to do something reprehensible or they are afraid they would get caught and jailed," I said.

"Correct. So, sometimes what seems good is not worth the risk of the bad that could come from it. It works the other way, too. Sometimes accepting bad *is* worth the good that comes from it," Grandma said.

That made sense to me too. I was starting to get it, but I still had questions.

Grandma smiled. "If everything were pleasure there would be no pleasure. One would simply begin to define pleasure within degrees and assign a preference to some degrees of pleasure over other degrees. The same is true of pain. We often connect the idea of pleasure as being good and pain as being bad but one must understand that pain is not a punishment and pleasure is not a reward. Pain and pleasure are simply different ends of the same spectrum or different sides of the same wheel. Consider the color blue. One might begin with a light blue and end up with a dark blue. It is not that light blue is better or that dark blue is better, there is no better. There are simply variations within the spectrum of the color blue. Do you understand the comparison?" Grandma asked.

"You are saying that pain is not necessarily bad and pleasure is not necessarily good. But, if that is true why does pleasure feel so good?" I asked.

"Ah, yes. Feelings," Grandma said smiling. She patted and rubbed my back for a moment. "Feelings come into existence when the human brain reacts to a stimulus by firing electronic impulses called emotions across the web of the human nervous system. There is a difference between the brain and the mind. The brain can be seen as the physical device, or portion of the physical body that houses the mind. The mind can be understood as the metaphysical or nonphysical portion of the body that houses the Spirit or the Soul. Once the brain has done its job of firing emotions across the nerves the mind then must decide how to observe or react to the emotions that the brain created," Grandma said.

I looked up into the sky and thought about what Grandma was saying. A silver hawk like bird winged silently across a sapphire blue expanse above us and glints of light reflected from its slowly moving wings.

"Feelings or emotions are also observed within a spectrum. One person might feel *good* and one might feel *great* and yet the two may be experiencing the same exact emotion but relating to or naming it differently. Not all emotions feel *good*. So does this mean that there are *good* emotions and *bad* emotions?" Grandma asked.

"If we should not judge emotions on how they make us feel, how should we judge them?" I asked.

"Why do you sense the need to judge the emotion at all? Why not simply experience the emotion and understand what you created or allowed within your Visit that elicited that particular emotional response?" Grandma asked.

"I don't know, I guess I thought everybody judges their emotions," I said.

"Do you choose to live your life in response to the method you think everybody uses?" Grandma asked.

I was tempted to feel something negative about the lesson I was learning here, and I knew I could choose that.

I realized that having the choice and recognizing the choice did not necessarily mean I should make that choice. I decided not to choose to experience negative emotions. Instead, I asked the question, "What about fear?"

"Fear is an emotion that people often tie to pain and even sometimes tie to pleasure," Grandma said.

"How should people handle fear?" I asked.

"Fear not. That which you fear has no power other than the power you give it," Grandma said.

"That's it? Just don't fear?" I asked.

"I did not say that it was easy, but it is possible," Grandma said.

I changed the topic. "Does God have a divine purpose for us?" I asked.

"Whatever a soul believes is true for that soul. I am saying that from my perspective God is one name a soul may attribute to the source of all that exists. You may choose a different perspective and for you that perspective would be true," Grandma said.

"I still don't understand," I said.

"I am saying that from my perspective there is a purpose and a reason for everything, everyone and every event. The term divine suggests the concept of that which is greater than any one of us individually, and yes, I believe that there is a great purpose, a universal purpose, a divine purpose, or even a Source purpose for each of us individually and for all of us collectively," Grandma said.

"Why do souls here use the terms planning and planting interchangeably?" I asked.

"On Earth if you want a garden, you must plant the seeds. Once planted, the seeds can grow into the plant they were designed to be, *if* you properly care for them. This is what we mean here when we speak of planning and planting. Planning is not simply getting an idea and having a vague plan to accomplish it, but rather the action of planting and caring for a plan from seed stage until it has grown into what you desire. Planting involves putting something that belongs to us into action to accomplish a specific task. The something we use is similar in nature to a seed. When we actively plant or plan an intended outcome, truth or event, it can begin to grow into reality," Grandma said.

Joan and Wally disappeared and Grandma led me up and over a little hill that seemed uneven in shape. There was a slight increase leading up the hill and a huge mountain looking down from the other side. On the way down the hill, we moved through a wandering path of gorgeous brightly colored flowers and the smell was sensational. Occasionally, I would stop along the way to touch the flowers. They felt soft, moist, luscious, and full of life. I heard birds singing and the sound of a babbling brook playing restfully. Tall lush trees were ablaze with a multitude of colors. They seemed to appear all around us as we wandered along the path. I began to see seagulls soaring overhead. They were gliding in the glorious light, raising and floating in simple yet exotic patterns. I saw a brook emerge as we turned a casual corner and the trees suddenly disappeared. At first, the brook seemed tiny but then it widened and I noticed that white foam formed as the brook bubbled upward away from the pool. I almost missed the fact that the laughing splashing water seemed to be running up hill. I looked again, but the scene around me was so comforting and peaceful that I shrugged off the oddity. Ocean waves seemed to emerge from one part of the brook while another part seemed invitingly shallow.

"Step into the water if you like," Grandma said.

I tested the water with one toe and found it soothingly pleasant. I stepped in and the sand at the bottom of it was like soft soothing gel and I sank an inch or two into its caress. I could almost taste the sweet flavor of the peace that drifted toward me in the waters embrace. I moved deeper into the pond and the water began to bubble and I was reminded of a time on Earth when I experienced a hot tub. The warm soothing water covered me from spiritual toes to spiritual waist and the pulsing of the water sent waves of relaxation and rest through my entire being. I felt cleansed and rested and I became comfortable and carefree. After a moment, the scene vanished and Grandma and I were back where we had been moments ago. I was learning to expect things to be different here and I didn't question the respite of the unusual pool.

"What is Purpose Tasking?" I asked.

Grandma only smiled in answer.

"Well, that is a very good question," Joan said suddenly appearing beside us.

As soon as Joan had communicated these words, Grandma disappeared.

"Don't worry. You can contact them or anyone else you like when ever you like," Joan said.

Paul L. Bailey

Chapter 9

Joan and I seemed to be standing outside an ancient city with high brick walls surrounding it. The city appeared to be rectangular and I was facing the narrow side. The walls of brick were similar in appearance to the brick around the fireplace in the Library. The bricks were pure white and many of them shone with a rainbow of colors seemingly boiling inside them. A door a hundred-feet tall and fifty-feet wide was open and a wide inverted bowl-shaped bridge made of silver and gold colored bricks, placed alternately, led into the city.

Unlike on Earth, I was able to stand close to the city's gate and see the entirety of the city. I saw all four of the city's walls and each of the six towers that stood spaced along the city's narrow sides. I saw the twelve towers that stood spaced along the wide sides. From this vantage point, the city appeared ancient. Standing here I could also see inside of the gate and the city appeared to be from the period I had most recently visited Earth. Twin skyscrapers stood one set in each of the four corners of the city. Each of these sets reminded me of the world trade center that had been destroyed on Earth date September 11, 2001.

Hundreds and hundreds of people were dancing around the outside of each set of towers. Everyone was rejoicing and celebrating the family and friends that they so loved and the lives that all of those family members and friends were so bravely living on Earth. There was a large screen and every family member of those that waited were shown going about their daily Earthly activities. A giant roar of joy erupted every time that a family member on Earth experienced laughter, because laughter helps to create the power of the Source of all that exists.

Each celebrant carried some reminder of their life on Earth before 9.11.01 in addition to reminders of the lives that they would surely live again on Earth. Most of those who had come Home on that day had chosen to wait here together at the replicas of the world trade center within the City of Choices. They waited for their loved ones and the loved ones of the others who were there. They knew that they would all come here when each had been to their own Hall of Review. Each of the celebrants was anxiously awaiting one of the greatest and most joyous reunions in the history of humankind.

Large pristine parks sporting grasses of green, purple, gold and silver were plentiful within the City. There were sporting facilities and stadiums in every section of the City. In the center of the City, hundreds of replicas of automobiles, trucks, buses, bicycles, motorcycles, trains, airplanes and other types of vehicles could be seen. Here many more people waited and celebrated the lives of their families and friends on Earth. Those who waited here were the thousands who left Earth unexpectedly as children as well as those who left Earth in vehicle accidents and all types of sporting events. Those gathered here rejoiced every time one on their family members or friends on Earth experienced true joy, because joy is also a part of the power of the Source.

The World Beyond: The Library on the Other Side

In the center of the city was a large building that reminded me of a hospital. Many more people waited here for their loved ones. Some of these people had left Earth after brave fights with illnesses and diseases of all kinds. Others had lost hope while on Earth and taken their own lives while still others had their life taken by the action of another. Each of these cheered for their loved ones and family members that remained on Earth and rejoiced in every smile that their loved ones experienced, because smiles, like laughter and joy help to create the power of the Source.

I asked Lucretia to continue with Joan on the tour and I went into the City of Choices to see what choices were there for me to make.

Once inside the City of Choices I noticed there were no traffic jams, no lighted traffic signals, no sounding vehicle horns and no trash on the streets. All the vehicles on the only city street were parked and motionless. There walls of the buildings were pristine and there was no graffiti, and no police officers. No one was addicted to drugs or alcohol. No one smoked cigarettes and no one was overweight. To my astonishment there were no Starbucks, no McDonalds and no retail stores.

A young man in a light grey business suit was standing near the entrance to the city. He wore a traditional white shirt and maroon tie and expensive looking brown shoes accented by an expensive looking gold plated watch. I began to wonder where he found such things in a city without restaurants, clothing stores and jewelry stores. The young man looked up at me and smiled and I heard his thoughts as clearly as I would have heard his words.

"Hello, Leena, My name is David. I was the little brother who left Earth at the end of six Earth years of the illness you call cancer," he said.

I had only vaguely remembered David since I had been only seven or eight years old when he had left Earth. Now I was meeting him here at Home, and the little boy I hardly remembered had grown into an attractive and well dressed young man.

"By now you must have realized that a soul may choose any sort of style of body or clothing they like. I have chosen these because they represent a well dressed and successful person in the most recent Visit that you experienced," David said.

I nodded and thought something about how nice he looked.

"There is no need to give false praise here. Here, you are most valued when you are simply who you are, no masks, no politically correct mannerisms, just be yourself," David said.

I nodded again and smiled. David smiled back.

We moved past several buildings including one that was similar to a nineteen hundreds era North American courthouse and another that reminded me of an ultramodern office building. We came to a building that was similar to a large sports arena and saw bleachers and chairs situated all around the upper levels. On the field in the center of the arena instead of a baseball diamond or a football field there was a large open grassy area divided by a variety of different colored grasses. The field contained blue grass, gold colored grass, white grass and grass of a rich purple color. In one section of the field souls were moving about the various colors of grass and selecting circular medallions that floated in air. In another section of the field, souls were selecting a variety of what looked like gold covered hand tools, while in yet other area, they were selecting a variety of what looked like miniature musical or technical instruments.

In one area of the field brightly wrapped packages that looked like gifts were scattered reminding me of a mixture of an Earth Christmas holiday and an Easter egg hunt. In another, common appliances like irons, washing machines, dishwashers and ovens were stacked neatly in columns that floated like balloons. One area contained what looked like a tall wall of bricks of various colors. The wall was multidimensional and hard to describe in words. It was a tall wall made of bricks that was inside of a wall, over a wall and behind a wall, yet all in one high wall. My attention was drawn to the wall of bricks because of all the unusual things that I saw these seemed the most unusual.

"Those are the bricks of task," said David.

"Oh, do you mean Purpose Tasking?" I asked.

"No, purpose tasking is an activity. These are simply the bricks that house the tasks. The purpose of each task is hidden within its brick. A soul may look at the activity or task of any individual brick by closely examining it but the actual purpose of the bricks activity is only discovered once the soul has committed to accomplish the task. You noticed some of these bricks in the Hall of Review – which you referred to as the Library on the Other Side. You nearly reached out to touch one, do you recall?" David asked.

"Yes, the brick that attracted my attention was a white brick that was glowing with a rose-colored light. I was going to reach for it, but a trumpet sounded and I began to focus on a scene outside the Library instead," I said.

"That was a brick of task that you once chose to accomplish." David said.

I looked at David and he smiled tenderly.

"It is easy to forget all of this when you first return from a Visit." David said.

I wasn't sure what he meant.

"You see, very near the time when a soul is born on Earth, their memory of the World Beyond is carefully hidden behind a vale of human thought so that they can truly learn the lessons they came to learn. The vale is thin at first, then as our Visit to Earth continues a vale of memory and a vale of experience overlap the vale of human thought making our memories of Home and our past lives almost invisible. We maintain only a sense we often refer to as déjà Vu. Here at Home we are capable of doing many things simultaneously. When you Visit Earth, everything that you are leaves here and takes up residence in the human body that you choose. Earth residents are allowed to see and directly and easily communicate with residents here in their early youth and again just before leaving Earth. While a young baby, a soul's Spirit Guide and other souls communicate with the child in the same language of thought that is used here. In case you are wondering, that explains to whom all of those babies are babbling. Most of the babies are not aware that they are vocalizing their thoughts until their parents or care givers begin to vocalize thoughts back to them using speech," he said.

I smiled and nodded. That seemed right to me.

"Most souls depart from the new Earth child as the child reaches his or her first or second birthday. Frequently a soul's Spirit Guide will remain during early childhood and continue to communicate and play with the child. This is where the idea of an imaginary playmate comes from. When the child has become convinced by other Earth residents that his or her Spirit Guide must be imaginary since only the child can see or hear them, the child often leaves behind the Spirit Guide and becomes engrossed in communicating only with other Earth residents. This explains why there is a process needed should the grown child desire to communicate with their Spirit Guide. That person must remember how to access a part of them that they closed in order to fit in with their human counterparts," he said.

I liked that thought too.

"I noticed that some of the bricks in the Library seemed to be closer to me, some pushed further away and others somewhere in between. Can you explain why?" I asked.

"The placement of the bricks can be a somewhat difficult thing to understand, so allow me to give you a somewhat simplistic explanation. Imagine that you are comparing the relationship between the placements of the bricks within the Hall of Records to the relationship of the placement of the planets within what some refer to as Earth's solar system. The solar system is another of the clues placed all around Earth residents as to the truth of things," David said.

I nodded hoping to encourage him to say more.

"Just as the planets are placed within a certain relationship to each other and move within predictable patterns, the bricks are placed within a relationship that can be called a circumstance circle. You have already learned a few things about circumstance circles and I can tell you that in the same way that the planets seem to revolve around the sun, the bricks revolve or circle the various active wheels within a soul's path. So, the placement of the bricks and their alignment or movement represents various concentric circumstance circles which rotate or develop within the development of soul's life wheels," David said.

"Are you saying that the bricks are a way of seeing how the different tasks I have chosen work together?" I asked.

"That is one way to envision it, but remember that we are speaking within a very simplistic explanation and not fully understanding the concepts involved," David said.

"Would it be of value for me to fully understand this concept at this point?" I asked.

"Perhaps the detailed answers to questions such as this one and the question you earlier asked about how a soul can relate someone in a physical body would be best answered when you have gained a better understanding of the truths currently before you," David said.

I nodded and accepted that idea, but it brought a different question to mind.

"Why would keeping the memory of the World Beyond make it more difficult to learn the lessons we went to Earth to learn?" I asked.

"Because the truth and certain knowledge of life beyond death would make certain lessons seem inconsequential. If you knew that nothing – even what you refer to as death could harm or alter your true being in any way – most people would have a very different perspective on their Visit. You likely saw a version of this occur when a person learned that they had a terminal illness. Suddenly the person can become very relaxed and at ease – because they believe that the end is near," he said.

I did recall an incident almost exactly like that from my life as Leena. I smiled.

"Besides, if a soul were to fully awake while on Earth, that soul could change things for hundreds if not thousands of years. Do you remember Jesus? He was a soul that was fully awake and thousands of years after he left Earth, Earth is still different because of him," David said.

"Why is it that many people on Earth seem to be searching for something?" I asked.

"Many times people seem to be in search of a purpose. Others are searching for meaning in their lives. Yet others, tend to idealize that which they perceive that they do not have," David said.

"They idealize what they do not have? What do you mean?" I asked.

"Picture an Earth resident that doesn't have much money. That person might idealize what it would be like to have a great amount of money. They may build an elaborate picture or dream of what it would be like to be wealthy. The more their actual circumstances exhibit not enough money, the bigger and better the dream of having money can become. The reality is that if the same person suddenly obtained a lot of money the reality of having it would not likely match the beautiful dream that the person created," David said.

"So, are you saying that the more a person wants something, the more they tend to idealize having it?" I asked.

"This is true for some people. The more people believe that there is a scarcity of something the more they want the thing. Their desire for the thing can sometimes become idealized. Once people believe that there is enough of something and that the thing is readily available to them, than the familiarity of the thing reduces its desire and the tendency to idealize it," he said.

I smiled. He had just explained something I had experienced first hand. When I was a child, I had loved rocky road chocolate ice cream. I couldn't ever seem to get enough of it. My brother Alan once bet me that I couldn't eat two gallons of the ice cream and I happily took him up on the wager. Alan bought the two gallons of the ice cream and I sat down to what I envisioned as heaven. The first few bowls full were wonderful but by the time I finished the first gallon I no longer wanted the ice cream and by the time I was half finished with the second gallon, I never wanted to see that flavor of ice cream again.

I changed the topic.

"Tell me about the bricks of task," I said.

"Part of what a soul decides here in the City of Choices is the answer to several questions: have you gained all of the experience and education you choose to gain within the wheels of Earth and similar places, or do you choose to Visit again? What do you choose as the central hub purpose for your next Visit or task? What portion of your overall purpose wheel should be dominated by your hub purpose? Is your next Visit primarily about learning lessons or gaining experiences? Are those lessons or experiences primarily to benefit you or chiefly to help others? If your Visit is largely to help others, are you willing to accomplish a specific task known as a purpose task so that a great many others may learn a valuable lesson? If you have accomplished enough purpose tasks, would you agree to incarnate as an element?" David said.

I nodded. I was eager to learn all about the various choices awaiting me.

"Many souls choose to learn lessons that involve what people on Earth call disasters. Some call these things Earthquakes, tornados, tsunamis, storms and floods. Others call these things, 'Acts of God.' The truth is that these things are the selfless acts of souls who choose to incarnate as these events so that others may have the experience of living through – or leaving Earth – by means of the event in question," David said.

"Do you mean to tell me that an Earthquake or hurricane is actually a soul carrying out a task?" I asked.

"That is one way to perceive the reality," David answered.

"Is there more than one way?" I asked.

"Things are not as they seem." David answered smiling.

"Yea, I've heard that a lot since I got here," I answered.

"Do you understand what it means?" David asked.

"Not really," I said.

"Each and every soul has within them the means to perceive any given event or circumstance in any manner that the soul chooses. Two souls may see a drunk in the street. One may perceive the drunk to be someone who is addicted and lost and miserable and in need of being rescued. Another soul may see the same drunk as someone who is free from the worries of everyday life, happy and content within his or her own mind and one to envy. In the end, the only opinion about the drunk that matters is what the drunk perceives about themselves," David said.

"Are you saying that there is no right or wrong way to perceive anything – and that is why things are not as they seem?" I asked.

"You have said it very well, Leena. There is no right or wrong way. There is only a way that seems right or wrong. Remember that right and wrong are judgments in the same way that good and evil are judgments. To the soul that judges a thing right, it is right. To the soul that judges a thing wrong, it is wrong. The same is true with good and evil," David said.

"What about those who are drunks or addicts, aren't they wasting their lives?" I asked.

"They are living the lives they have chosen. If they choose to stop living their life as a drunk or an addict all they need is to actively work at it and they will stop. But if they choose to continue that type of life as something that is worthwhile to the soul who chose it, then it is never wasted," David said.

"But, shouldn't people help those who are down and out?" I asked.

"Help is only beneficial if the person in question believes themselves to be down and out and if they desire help," David said.

"I've heard a lot about the importance of what a person believes. Can you explain it to me?" I asked.

"A person is as that person believes him or herself to be," David said.

"Run that by me one more time," I requested.

"If you are dressed in poor person's clothes, live in a poor person's house, and do the work of a poor person, are you rich or poor?" David asked.

"Poor, I guess," I said.

"It does not matter how others view a person. If the person views their condition as poor, then that person is poor. If the person views their condition as rich, then the person is rich. It does not matter how large the number is in a bank account but rather how the person views the number. One person may see the sum of one million dollars in a bank account and see themselves as rich while another may see the same amount as an indication that they are poor. The same is true of any other judgment," David said.

"You are saying that the only person who can say if a person is rich or poor, happy or sad, successful or unsuccessful is the person themselves," I said.

"This is one way to perceive it," David said.

Then I saw another soul, and I knew him at once. Seth stood leaning casually against the glimmering silver glass like wall of a large office type building. An empty bus sat stopped at a crosswalk in front of the building. Above the bus I saw the only traffic signals I had seen here, but the signals were not lighted. Seth wore the same kind of holed jeans and dingy untied tennis shoes he had worn when I last saw him alive on Earth. Now he stood with his back against a wall, his feet crossed and reading a newspaper. He looked both comfortable and carefree.

Chapter 10

David disappeared and Seth spoke to me in the now familiar language of thought.

"What sup Ma?" he asked.

"Seth," I exclaimed.

"I figured you'd find me here," he said.

"Do you mean here on the other side, or here at this building?" I asked.

"Yep," he said nodding his head.

"What happened?" I asked a bit confused by his answer.

"Never saw the dumb bus," Seth said with his head hung.

I smiled. I had guessed as much.

"I was jus' walkin' to Mickey D's for a bite. I had to cross the street but I was'n' payin' attention and never saw it 'till after it hit me," he said.

"*After* it hit you?" I asked.

"Yep. I floated up out-ah my body and saw the dumb bus parked on me. The back left wheel of it was jus' sittin' on my chest! Knew I was dead before I realized Marshall was there with me. Marshall said I walked into the side of the bus and was pulled under its back tire," he said.

"Marshall?" I asked.

"He's my Spirit Guide. I chose to stay here at this age to meet yah. Figured you'd like it," Seth said.

"Seth, do you understand this place?" I asked.

"Yea, but do ya mind if I switch my appearance 'for I start answerin' questions?" he asked.

"That will be fine," I said.

Seth instantly took on the appearance of an adult in his mid thirties. His teenage ragged jeans and holed tennis shoes were gone and in their place was a nice pair of white slacks and a beautiful wine and gold colored jacket. Well-shined dress black loafers replaced the grimy tennis shoes. Several gold chains hung from his neck and he sported a diamond like earring in a gold setting. His formerly shaggy and unkempt hair now appeared neatly barbered and combed. I did a bit of a double take. On Earth one watches their children grow up over a period of time, here I had just watched Seth grow up in seconds. But that wasn't right either. He hadn't grown up in seconds – because here there were no seconds. Here there was no time.

Seth smiled. "Relax, Mom. It will all make sense to you."

"This building is sort of the first stop for newcomers to the City of Choices. It is the UCC building - Ultimate Choice Center building, that is. Would you like to go in?" he asked.

I looked up at him with pride and smiled. He took my arm and escorted me into the building.

We stopped at a reception desk. The soul behind the desk was a well-dressed middle-aged woman. She looked up at us and handed us each two white circular discs. One disk said Home and the other said Experience. The Experience side was twinkling on both Seth's disc and on my own. I looked at Seth and he held up the one that said Experience and I did the same.

"Fine," the woman soul said. Then she gave us each a file that contained a variety of multicolored folders. I opened my file and saw folders entitled 'Servant/Master', 'Healer/Disease", 'Entertainer/Privacy' and 'Unplanned'. Only the one titled Unplanned was not twinkling. I looked over at Seth's folders and noticed these were entitled 'Leader/Follower', 'Labor/Ease", 'Lawful/Unlawful' and 'Unplanned'. "Choose one file each," she said.

I picked 'Entertainer/Privacy' and Seth chose 'Leader/Follower'.

"You have selected the primary purpose wheel for your next Visit. Move along," she said.

Just past her desk, it seemed that we had somehow ended up back outside again and we stood at a crossroads. There were signs identifying each of the paths and two or three of the paths were twinkling. I glanced at them.

"These signs are from the Planners. They have suggested a few different paths for you to consider. You are free to ignore the suggestions of the Planners and choose your own way, but I wouldn't recommend it. The Planners understand elements of Home and Earth that you and I may not yet have recognized and their suggestions are always for the best benefit of you and others," Seth said.

I decided to follow the recommendations of the Planners and found myself standing with Seth at a rectangular table filled with thousands of circular shaped pieces of material made out of some type of mirrored glass. A soul could pick up each piece, look into it and see themselves in their next task or incarnation. I picked up a piece of glass and Seth took it away from me. "First you need an explanation of the process. If you will look carefully at each glass before picking it up you will notice that several carry your reflection. The Planners have selected these as the best possible matches for your next incarnation or task," he said.

I looked at the pieces and saw reflections not only of myself as Leena, but also reflections of myself as Lucretia and many other lives or Visits. Each view of my body was surrounded with a ring of silver, gold, blue, green or purple clouds. Then I noticed that each of the reflections had many common elements. In each I was female, had light colored hair and stood about the same height. Each face had similar traits as if they were all sisters or cousins from the same large family.

"Don't rely too much on the appearance of your body. Instead, look at the purpose of each Visit or task," Seth suggested.

I wondered why he was making that comment when I heard his thoughts interrupt my own.

"You are viewing versions of your body that you have chosen in other visits. If you choose to incarnate again, you will make a choice of a body for your next Visit at the Body Mall," he said.

By now I had learned not to get too upset by concepts I didn't understand. There was more that I didn't understand about the World Beyond than there was that I did. I looked at several of the glasses and in each I was pictured in front of a large group of people playing a musical instrument or singing. In a few I was an actor or I was a model. I selected the glass that showed me playing a musical instrument or singing. Seth had found glasses with very different activities. He was a high-ranking military officer or he was a ships captain. He was the CEO of a large company or he was a politician. He was a Real Estate investor or he was a corrupt leader. Seth chose the glass that pictured him as either a military officer or a ships captain and we found ourselves on the uniquely colored grass of the stadium. From among the musical instruments I chose two; a soloists singing voice and a piano. A Planner waved a hooded sleeve and the piano became smaller and the singing voice became larger. I nodded in agreement. Seth chose between the military and a trade ship captain and he chose the military. He also chose to be a captivating speaker with a magnetic personality.

I was momentarily separated from Seth and stood in a room that reminded me of a grade school auditorium. There were dozens of photographs and recordings of singers from across Earth history. I stood amazed at the number of choices that were before me and decided to create my own mixture of a voice with elements from each of my favorite performers. I mixed a little of Sippie Wallace's blues with a little Clara Smith blues styling. I added some of Jane Bathori classical sound to Kathleen Ferrier opera styling. I picked a healthy helping of Tammy Wynette's country sound and added a portion of Violeta del Carmen Parra Sandoval's folk music and I added a dash of Dinah Washington's gospel blues and a dose of Billy Holiday's and Nina Simone's jazz styling. I picked a little of Judy Garland's stage presence, added a little Rosemary Clooney's simple vocal beauty with a dash of Ethel Merman's throaty vibrato. I added a bit of Ruth Etting's pop styling to some Bessy Smith blues. Then I got excited and added a little Ethel Waters styling and presence to a little of Josephine Baker's presentation and vocal range. With this voice, I should be able to sing almost anything and do it well.

Joan appeared and I was back with Seth. She told us that the most important portion of our choices had been completed. She suggested that we each leave ourselves in the City of Choices and to also go to the Body Mall. I decided to leave two of me at the City of Choices. One of me was there to complete the remainder of the choices that needed to be made and another was there to create a replica of the Road Star and wait beside it for Lee's arrival. For that me, I chose to wear the same clothing as I had been wearing on the day of the motorcycle accident. For the me that remained in the City of Choices to make choices I was comfortable with the white tunic I had found myself wearing at the Library. I chose a gorgeous multidimensional multicolor dress to visit the Body Mall.

I thought how nice it would have been to have this ability on Earth. There could be one of me to stay with the kids and another to go to work. One of me could go shopping and another could travel. They even had a name for that on Earth, they called it cloning. But here there were no clones. Here I could have as many of me as I could use, and each of me was truly me. Even now there were two of me at the Library reviewing my own Visits, two more of me reviewing the Visits of others, two of me at the City of Choices and one of me on my way to the Body Mall with Seth, and it all seemed as normal as a day shopping and enjoying the smell of new shoes at a mall on Earth.

Paul L. Bailey

Chapter 11

The body mall was unlike any other mall I had ever seen. It was situated in a lovely country atmosphere with rolling hills and unfenced grazing livestock that were unbothered by flies or pests. There was a feeling of being a hundred miles from the nearest town and the simple beauty of a relaxed and unhurried pastoral setting. The exterior of the mall reminded me of a sprawling ranch in the heartland of America. Old whitewashed buildings stood lazily clustered together in a clearing across dozens of miles as far as the eye can see. The buildings seemed weathered as if they had been constructed a century ago. I scanned the scene with a sense of wonder and noticed that many things seemed to be missing. The large bright red barns together with their haylofts, the rusty dusty decades old tractor standing hood open and smelling of oil, grime and fuel fumes. Barking dogs and crowing roosters; all of these things were missing. I realized that the things I was looking for were features of an Earth country setting and would be as unlikely to find here, as a pond with fish swimming above it would be to find there.

I heard the distant cry of a birdcall and it seemed to be the only sound other than the pleasant song of an early morning's sunrise in silence. Here in the midst of it all stood this simple looking unpretentious ranch whose building and barns served as the malls stores. A solitary man stood in the distance adorned in coveralls with a red patterned handkerchief partially stuffed into his back pocket. He was bare foot and chewing on a long piece of golden straw. He wore a straw hat and a serene expression as he gazed at the scene before him. He turned and beckoned me to come and I moved toward him.

He explained that I had before me many choices relating to the body, vessel or vehicle I would choose to carry my Soul through its next Visit. He explained that once a soul chooses the various elements, they may view their chosen body at four stages of growth; Earth age twelve, age twenty-one, age thirty-five and fifty years of age. The man led us to the front door of the first store, which was the height and weight store. Here a soul could choose from all of the different height and weight combinations for their next Visit. The store had large windows that reminded me of a story I remembered about a five and dime store chain's rise and fall. The mannequins, if that is what they were, consisted of legs, midsection and torso. All were without arms, feet and heads yet; I could have sworn that they were aware that we were there.

Some mannequins moved from side to side while others seemed to jump up and down. I glanced over at Seth but he seemed not at all amazed by the display window. A sign above the store continually spoke the name of the store as each Soul passed by.

"Welcome to Height and Weights Unlimited," the sign said again and again.

A jolly portly gentleman in black top hat and tails greeted us as we stepped into the store and the man who had shown us the way disappeared. The jolly gentleman pointed us toward one of several rectangular tan colored tables in the center of the rustic store. The simple wooden tables each contained a device that reminded me of a laptop computer. I stood before one laptop and Seth chose the one next to mine.

"Greetings Leena," the device said.

I just looked at the device without comment until Seth leaned over and motioned for me to answer.

"Hello?" I asked tilting my head as if speaking into a speaker telephone.

"Would you like to view all of the height and weight combinations you have chosen in Visits to Earth?" It asked.

I indicated that I would like that and the computer, or whatever it was, quickly brought up a multi-dimensional graph that showed each of the bodies I had chosen for other Visits. The graph managed to simultaneously show height and weight at each of four separate ages as viewed from all sides from hundreds of different bodies. The only things missing from the views of the various bodies were the feet, arms, hands and head. These were blacked out or grayed out. They were represented, but not viewed. I reviewed my previous height and weight combinations and then noticed three combinations for my next Visit each twinkling in the way that the book I had earlier read in the Library had twinkled. I now understood that the twinkling was a method employed by the Planners to indicate choices that would be to my best advantage and to the best advantage of the lessons I would learn on my next Visit. The Planners had in mind what was best for me and suitable for my purpose, so I chose one of the combinations that they suggested. My purpose was Entertainer/Privacy and I chose a suitable height and weight. The combination I chose would make me considerably taller and substantially thinner than Leena had been and I preened in the view of my new more aesthetically pleasing body.

I looked to see what Seth had chosen. Seth had chosen to be tall and muscular. The ladies would consider him a hunk. It was a perfect combination for his Visit as a military officer. Seth had been a short stocky boy in his last incarnation, so for him his new choice was as different as my own.

Once we had each made our selections, we were given another opportunity to change any aspect of our height or weight. Seth and I had chosen carefully and neither of us opted for any revisions. The jolly gentleman that had shown us into the store gave us each a small disc that contained a hologram of the height weight combination we had chosen. We stepped from the store and I noticed that several of the other shoppers had activated their holograms so that the unusual sight of headless, armless bodies seemed to be walk-floating just behind or just ahead of the soul that had chosen it.

Seth and I arrived at the next store by means of thought travel and I wondered if people on Earth would enjoy this form of travel. It would certainly put a number of large companies out of business. All that was needed to go to any destination was to visualize where you wanted to go, and you were there. The travel took place instantaneously and physical distance did not seem to matter. The Planners took care of all of the details.

I looked at the next store and it was, well, watching us. There were numerous pairs of disembodied eyes looking out from all of the windows near the entrance. Ears were also perched in the windows and apparently using a crawling technique to move within the window. They were apparently listening to what was being said aloud and I wondered if they heard much since almost all communication here was by thought. Various hair colors, textures and styles were also visible at the windows. These took the appearance of wigs that floated through the air and the totality of the window display was unusual to say the least.

Seth and I entered the store and were this time welcomed by a tall thin man dressed as a farmer. He held a device that reminded me of a combination shovel and sickle in one hand and used the other to direct us to a table that was shaped like a human eye and chairs shaped like human ears. I noticed that although he appeared to be dressed as a farmer he also seemed to be dressed in the hooded white tunic I had seen so often. It seemed strange at first that a person could be dressed in two different outfits at the same time and then I remembered that if I could see all of me each of me would be wearing a different outfit.

My attention was directed to the left sleeve of the farmer's tunic and there I saw the three dimensional representation of a hand sewing seeds. I looked up at the farmer and noticed that his eyes were each a different color. One eye was silver and the other was gold. It was unusual and I thought of asking about it, but I became distracted with everything else that was going on. I went to the laptop computer type device and noticed that it resembled human hair and it spoke to each of us and asked if we would like to review the eye, ear and hair combinations we had chosen for other incarnations. Seth chose sandy blond hair and deep blue eyes and small tidy ears while I chose my usual red hair, green eyes and large ears.

After Seth and I finished making our choices, the eyes, ears and hair colors and textures were added to our holograms. The man dressed as a farmer looked at me strangely but he said nothing.

"Did you see the way that farmer looked at me?" I asked Seth as we left the store.

"Oh, he's a Planner. I think he expected you to choose one of the twinkling color combinations for your hair and eyes, but you decided not to. That's all right; it's your choice," he said.

It was only then that I realized that other color combinations had been twinkling. I had consciously chosen to ignore them and choose my usual color combination. I had made a choice that had not been suggested by the Planners.

"Seth, what *are* the Planners?" I asked.

"The Planners are Souls who have moved forward beyond Visits to places like Earth. They have become very familiar with these places and the lessons that can be learned there. Now, the Planner's job is to plan the details of each life or Visit. That is actually the use for the concept known as time. The Planners use time to plan every second of every person's life. They plan every thought, every action, every idea, every concept, everything. When they are finished planning, they share the plan with the soul who will incarnate. Each Soul must agree to every single second of their planned Visit. If a soul does not agree to everything, the soul can either re-plan that particular thing or the Planners will plan it all again differently to meet the soul's needs and desires. A soul can change any aspect they choose right up to the time they begin the process called birth," Seth said.

"Do we always follow the plan once we are on Earth?" I asked.

"No. We often choose to create and follow other paths. No matter which paths we follow the planners keep trying to bring us back to a point where we can choose to reenter our choices if we want to," Seth said.

"And if we choose not to follow the choices we make here?" I asked.

"Then we create an unplanned path and follow it, but the Planners do not give up easily. They keep bringing us back to the point where we can choose to follow our purpose and plan," Seth said.

"It seems that the Planners do most of the planning. Why do we just go along with it?" I asked.

"We plan the significant aspects of our life and the lessons we plan to learn. The Planners take care of all the small details, and we have final veto power to change those details before we leave," Seth said.

"I was wondering, this place all seems to exist in the three dimensional realm of Earth while the other places

I've visited clearly existed in a multidimensional realm. Do you know why?" I asked.

"This is part of the City of Choices. You have chosen, either consciously or unconsciously to view it in three dimensions. It is your choice," Seth said shrugging.

Seth and I came to a store that seemed to be shaped like a human nose and mouth. You could move through either the nose or the mouth to enter the store – and Seth and I both chose to enter by means of the mouth. That turned out to be a significant choice because in so deciding we had each chosen to favor our mouth and allow our nose to be selected by our parents. If we had chosen to enter by means of the nose I assumed that the opposite would be true and our parents would select the size and shape of our nose, mouth and lips. We made our choices and the nose and mouth were added to our holograms.

Seth and I visited several other stores and selected other aspects of our appearance. The Planners carefully recorded each of our choices and coordinated our choices with the choices of others. When a group of souls made similar appearance choices, the Planners put the group together into a type of family to determine which portion of Earth they will Visit.

When we had exited the last store in the mall our holograms were complete and our new bodies were ready for the final touches of family that would be added in the City of Planning.

Chapter 12

Seth and I were just outside the City of Planning when Joan met up with us again. She communicated that Lee Woods had grown very old and was soon to arrive at Home. I sent one of me back to be present as Lee left Earth and left the other ones of me at their various tasks. Seth and I went on to the City of Planning, but I think I'll tell first about leading Lee Woods Home.

Joan introduced me to Mark, Lee's spirit guide and then Joan went about her other tasks. I learned that Mark had been Lee's spirit guide for the last four Visits just as Joan had been my own for the past five Visits. Each spirit guide had a number of souls for which they served simultaneously. This was simple for the spirit guides, since they were capable of multidimensional activities, another way of saying they could do more than one thing and be at more than one place at a time. Those of us who return to Earth would have to give up our multidimensional abilities while we were incarnate. Spirit guides could move between many of us and still seem to be constantly with us all since they reside at Home, but work with those of us on Earth.

I went with Mark into the Earth realm and since this trip had been planned it went very smoothly.

When we arrived Lee was sitting in a wheelchair in a nursing facility. Lee's body had Parkinson's disease and he had been in the wheelchair for two Earth years. Lee saw Mark first and I was reminded of how I felt when I had first seen Joan as I prepared to leave Earth. The Planners allowed some people who were in their final days on Earth to see souls who had already left Earth and when I appeared to Lee his crippled face found a way to smile. Mark asked Lee if he was ready to go and since Lee was also permitted to communicate by thought there was no hesitation on his part at all. Mark lifted Lee out of his broken body and I took Lee's spirit hand. Lee saw the spiral tunnel and the bright light and Mark and I traveled beside Lee until he entered the garden. I understood that it would be best for Lee not to see me again until he had experienced the twinkling books in his Hall of Review, so I left only a form of myself that was within a dimension that Lee could not yet comprehend. In this way I could be with Lee and still not interrupt an important occasion of review for him. Seth joined me and we sat together and watched the scene unfold.

Lee came through his garden and stood looking around his Library. I understood that Lee would learn to refer to it by its actual name, the Hall of Records. But by whatever name, it was very much as mine had been except that the colors were different. His colors were much more dark and masculine. Where my bookshelves had been translucent white his were deep cherry wood brown. Where the fireplace in my Library had had white and gold bricks, his bricks were red and gray. Then I understood that Lee was visualizing this place from his own perspective, just as I had perceived my own Library from my perspective.

The World Beyond: The Library on the Other Side

I watched as one of Lee's books began to twinkle and saw him reach for the book. I noticed that the door that Lee had entered the Library through had closed and disappeared almost as soon as he was through it and Lee never even glanced toward where the door had been. He evidently had no need to see his own funeral. He had no young children to be concerned about and he had been seemingly alone. I knew that he had never been truly alone. I knew that Mark had gone to sit with him constantly and many others spent time watching him from the City of Glass.

Lee opened the first twinkling book and found himself standing in a small simple inexpensive one bedroom apartment from the early nineteen fifties. Lee understood that he was seeing through the eyes of Edward Lee Woodworth. Edward was a young man at the end of yet another part-time job looking for a career. For weeks, he had been searching the largest daily paper in Oregon for an opportunity. A small ad in the Sunday Journal had caught his eye.

"Retail chain seeks ambitious career minded individual for management position."

The chain was a well-established five and dime store with locations all across the West Coast and Mid West of the United States. Most of the chain's stores were in larger cities and some cities had four or five locations. Edward lived in Portland, the largest city in Oregon and there were four stores there.

Edward dressed in his Sunday best suit and rode Rosy, the city bus to the busy downtown store. The brick exterior of the building suddenly looked more daunting than it had when Edward had shopped here as a child. The tall windows were each decorated in themes from the various departments including fashion, fabric and lingerie. A part-time window dresser came in once each week to update the windows. The man stood in a window now pulling a housedress over a currently bald mannequin. He was so involved in his work that he didn't notice Edward or any of the customers as they walked by or looked into the unfinished window.

Edward stood just outside the main door, straightened his tie, cleared his throat and walked deliberately into the main entrance. Edward made his way to the elevator and looked at the buttons. He paused a moment, took a deep breath and reached over and pushed the button labeled Office. Nothing at all happened for a full minute and Edward briefly wondered if the lift was out of order. Then, as if grudgingly, the elevator doors began to slide closed with a decisive squeak. Edward looked down at his shiny shoes as the elevator rose and he waited for the door to open.

From the open elevator door, Edward could see that the office consisted of a long hallway with many doors on either side. Edward stepped out of the elevator and looked around. On his right side was a glassed-in area where a middle-aged woman in a blue dress sat answering one telephone call after another. She saw Edward and held up a hand like a traffic officer and then slowly folded all but her index finger. Edward got the message and stood there waiting. The woman pushed a few more buttons, reversed the position of her hand and used the single index finger to beckon him toward her. She pushed the headset away from her left ear and lifted her eyes to meet his gaze smiling as he approached.

"Mr. Woodworth?" she asked.

"Yes. I have an appointment with Mr. Melvin," Edward answered.

Edward rolled his eyes at himself. Of course, he had an appointment. She knew who he was; she had called him by name.

"Mr. Melvin is on the telephone. Go on in and have a seat," the woman said with a stiff smile.

She pointed her long slim finger towards Melvin's office. Edward walked towards the doorway and heard a man's voice quietly speaking on the telephone. He crossed the threshold and Mr. Melvin looked up at him. Melvin was a busy looking man in a dark blue suit and a bright red and gray tie an inch below his neck. His brown hair, graying at the temples, was combed to perfection and he had the appearance of authority. He motioned Edward to a plain white metal folding chair near Melvin's plain white metal desk. Edward noticed small dents and bare metal spots marring the fronts of the desk and matching filing cabinets.

Melvin shook his head at the person on the other end of the telephone conversation and said, "No, no, no, no… that won't." Then without saying another word, he hung up the phone and turned to Edward.

"Mr. Edward Woodworth," Melvin exclaimed.

"Yes sir," Edward answered.

"Well, Mr. Woodworth what brings you to McKnight Stores?" Melvin asked.

"Mr. Melvin, I am interested in the management position you have open," Edward said.

"Umm," said Melvin noncommittally. "This job requires a five-day-a-week rotating schedule. The person we hire will work a minimum of forty-eight hours a week. I need someone that is a fast starter. I need an ambitious person. I need someone willing and able to go the distance. Does that sound like you?"

Edward answered in the affirmative.

Melvin shook his head sadly. "Alright you'll be on a fourteen day trial period. If at anytime during the fourteen days that I see you are not the man for the job, you're gone. If you survive for fifteen days – you're hired. Agreed?" Melvin asked.

Edward was stunned at the speed of Melvin's decision. He hadn't been in his office for five minutes.

Nevertheless, Edward managed a crooked smile. "Sure!" Edward said.

"Be here tomorrow morning at seven a.m. If you arrive after seven-oh-five forget about coming up here because you're fired. See you tomorrow," Melvin said.

Edward was almost certain that the telephone did not ring but Melvin picked it up anyway. Melvin started speaking immediately.

"…won't do at all. We'll have to plan another course," Melvin was saying.

Edward sat there a moment looking bewildered and Melvin raised one hand and waived him from the office as if Edward were an annoying fly. Edward walked from the office and exited into the busy store.

When Edward walked into Mr. Melvin's doorway at six-thirty the next morning Melvin was already sitting behind his desk. A tall dark haired man about five years older than Edward was seated in the metal chair he had occupied yesterday. Melvin glanced at Edward and then glanced at the clock. He looked up at Edward and frowned.

"You're late," Melvin said. Melvin tossed Edward a small plastic item. Ed caught it and turned it over. It was a well-used name tag that read, "McKnight Stores – Trainee".

"This is Mr. Rick Young. You will call him Mr. Young," Melvin said.

Edward walked toward Mr. Young with a hand extended but Young did not move from his chair nor did he turn to face him or acknowledge Edward in any way. Mr. Melvin looked at Mr. Young and seemed to grow a full two inches. Melvin spoke softly as if both filled with pride and struck with awe.

"Mr. Young is waiting for the call," Melvin said smiling like a proud father.

At this, Young stood erect as if at the military position of attention. The odd ritual visibly confused Edward and he glanced toward the back of Mr. Young's head and then to the telephone on Mr. Melvin's desk. He was curious what "call" Mr. Young was waiting for. Melvin looked back toward Edward and visibly shrunk. Melvin glanced at Young and said, "Pulls, Floor and Cash."

Edward wondered if he were going to meet members of an accounting firm or a legal firm. He didn't have long to wonder. Mr. Young turned toward Edward and looked at his shoes. Young's eyes traveled slowly up from Edward's shoes and by the time his eyes arrived at Ed's shoulders the disappointment painted on his face was as clear as his cold sea green eyes.

Young grabbed a three-inch stack of papers from a plastic tray and muttered, "Follow," in Edward's direction. Then Young nearly ran from the office. Edward hurried to follow Young through a maze of hallways and down a steep staircase. The hallway was tall and the sound of their hurried steps echoed like tiny pistol shots. Somewhere near the bottom step, Young spoke to Edward without bothering to look his direction. Young's voice rang with a hollow sound in the empty staircase.

"Use these," said Young. He grabbed the door handle, wrenched it open and hurried toward a darkened stockroom. Edward looked around to remember the location of the staircase. The hallway was painted faded green on the bottom and a dingy cream color on top. A bare bulb hung from the ceiling protected only by a metal looking cage. A long string hung limply from the light fixture. Young reached another wide doorway and pulled a wheeled table away from the wall. Young handed Edward about half of the stack of papers in his hand and muttered "Pull these," Edward had worked a summer as a warehouseman so he went to work comparing the item numbers from the pull sheet to the boxes stacked in the stock room. Edward worked quickly and finished his pulls before Young and went to help Young. Young looked up at him and his face registered a little less disgust as they pushed the two carts from the room and toward a freight elevator.

Young selected a button and they rode down in a jerky motion. Young pointed to four nearly empty square tables and mumbled, "Condense those to one table, and fill the other three – four items to a table. Stack 'em high." The task was easy once Edward looked around to the other similar tables. Young finished his work before Ed had finished his this time and Young came to watch him finish filling the last two items on a table. When Edward had finished Young again grunted, "Follow" and rushed off.

Young and Edward moved rapidly through aisle after aisle of merchandise on the lower level then they ran up the stairs and did the same until they had covered all of the floors. When the two men had finished Young asked, "Got it?" and Edward shook his head in the affirmative although he was only partly convinced that he understood what Young meant. Edward thought that this hurried trip through the floors was supposed to teach him the general layout of the store. He now had some idea of which departments were on each floor. He knew that if Young ever stopped for a lunch break he would have to walk the floors again more slowly and he would take notes in the small notepad that Edward had purchased and that now sat empty and ready inside his suit coat pocket.

Edward followed Young back down the stairs to the main floor while he turned on the remainder of the florescent lights and then began unlocking the doors. A few people stood waiting outside each door and filed in within seconds of having the doors open. Moments later the piped in orchestrated music that played slowed down versions of songs that had been popular a decade ago cracked and stopped. The hollow sound of a woman's voice over a load speaker said "Mr. Young to cash-wrap two." There was another cracking sound and the music started once again. Young hurried towards the check stand at the opposite end of the floor and Edward followed close behind him. Young reached for the intercom, pushed the blue button, and said, "Mr. Young". He listened for a moment, hung up the intercom and turned to the well-dressed woman working the check-stand. "Show and tell," Young said. Young turned to Edward and said, "Watch and learn," In a flash Young was gone from sight.

Edward introduced himself to the middle-aged thin woman. She gave him a half smile and introduced herself as Doreen. A customer arrived at the cash-wrap and Doreen said a cheerful "Good Morning!" to the customer and began ringing up the purchase. Edward watched Doreen ring up the next two customers. Then she turned to him and said, "It's my break, just go ahead and do as I showed you." Edward moved to the cash register and had only a moment to look directly at the keys before his first customer came up.

"Good Morning," Edward said and he began carefully ringing up the sale. Edward worked customer after customer. Fifteen minutes passed, then twenty and Doreen did not return. He thought about calling Mr. Young on the intercom but every time he started to do so another group of customers would appear at the cash-wrap. A frantic looking woman pushing a baby carriage was next in line. She handed Edward a large assortment of baby items and tended to the baby and another small child that stood holding the side of the baby carriage. When Edward had finished ringing up her purchase, she handed him two twenty-dollar bills for a nineteen-dollar seventy-cent total purchase. Edward pushed the second twenty back towards her and handed her the thirty cents in change. She absently took the thirty cents and walked away leaving the other twenty-dollar bill lying on the counter. Edward called to her, "Madam, you forgot your change". She turned back, accepted her money, and left the store. A few moments later both Mr. Young and Doreen were back at the cash-wrap. Young told Edward to balance the cash drawer by leaving exactly the amount that had been there at the start of the day in the drawer and to pull the remainder. The two men walked back to the office and Young went to talk to Mr. Melvin while Edward counted the cash. According to the x-report, there was exactly $5.04 too much in the bag. Edward showed Mr. Young and Mr. Melvin both the report and the extra cash. Melvin smiled and said, "Okay. You passed the first test. Now take an hour for lunch and come back ready to work," Melvin and Young turned and walked back into the office and Edward took out his notepad and walked down to the lower level to start taking merchandise location notes.

The remainder of the first day seemed to stretch out in an endless progression of lessons about the retail trade and when Edward arrived at the office at six a.m. the next morning he found that Mr. Young and Mr. Melvin were not there yet. Edward smiled and left a note on Mr. Melvin's desk telling him where he was, emptied the pull list drawer and went to the storeroom. By the time that Mr. Young came into the storeroom, Edward had finished the pulls and was moving the carts toward the elevator. Young and

Edward filled the empty tables and by eight o'clock, and they were back in Mr. Melvin's office.

"Care to join us for morning coffee Mr. Woodworth?" Melvin asked smiling.

Edward nodded his head and the three men took the small passenger elevator to the main floor. Edward learned that on most weekdays the management staff would meet here in the coffee shop for a brief meeting at ten o'clock. Melvin introduced Edward to Mr. Hanes, the assistant manager in charge of the lower level and Mrs. Boyce, the assistant manager in charge of the main level. Just then, a familiar looking young woman came towards our table. She was the woman that had left the twenty-dollar bill lying on the cash-wrap. Mr. Melvin turned to her and introduced her to Edward as Ms. Tanner, the assistant manager in charge of the third floor.

"It's very important that the management staff can be trusted with cash," Melvin explained.

"I'm glad you passed the test, you seem nice," Tanner said.

"Were those your children?" Edward asked.

"No, they are my older sister's kids. I borrow them every time we hire a new trainee."

Edward shrugged his shoulders. He understood the reasons for the test and it was nice to prove to everyone, including himself that he could be trusted with money.

During the meeting Mr. Hanes talked about total sales on the lower level the previous day and mentioned the items that were selling best. Mr. Young gave the numbers for the second floor and Ms. Tanner gave the third floor report. Mrs. Boyce talked about the coffee shop and the special that was currently running on iced tea. The tea was inexpensive to produce and was sold as, "All you can drink," for forty-nine cents. Most folks would drink only one ten-ounce glass with their meal. A few would down two glasses and the profit would still be high. The store would make a profit even if a customer drank seven ten-ounce glasses of iced tea, few did.

Edward sat looking towards the lunch counter and noticed what in those days was called a bum. The bum was wearing tattered and faded denim pants and a dirty-yellowed t-shirt. His hair was caked with so much dirt it was impossible to determine the natural color. He sat at the lunch counter drinking the all-you-can-drink iced tea. Each time he would guzzle the tea and a gush of yellow liquid would appear near his right shoe. The more tea he drank, the larger the yellow puddle became. Mr. Young, Mr. Hanes, Mr. Melvin and Edward all rose from the table and quickly escorted the man from the store. He did not protest until the men released him outside of the Fifth Street door. Then he turned to the four men and complained "But it said all ya' can drink, and I was still drinkin', yeah?"

The next days passed quickly as Edward was briefly shown task after task. He learned how to handle the seemingly countless tasks of running a retail store. Edward even learned that *waiting for the call* meant that Mr. Young was ready for his first store assignment and only waiting until a store was available for him. Edward had been so busy that when Mr. Melvin called him into his office it seemed as if Edward had only been working there a few days. Edward was surprised when Melvin handed him a key to the store and a name tag that read McKnight Stores, Mr. Woodworth, Assistant Manager.

"Woodworth you have survived for fifteen days. Congratulations. Now get back to work," Melvin picked up his telephone and Edward knew the meeting was over. He was hired. If only Edward had known then what he learned later he would have run from the store and never come back.

The page went blank and another page began to twinkle. Lee turned to the page and found himself five years later in Edward's life. Edward had been rapidly promoted to his first store and then shortly thereafter to his second. He had married his high school sweetheart Leslie Marley, a sweet dark-haired blue-eyed beauty that had captured his heart from the moment he saw her. Two years later Edward had been handed his dream job, District Manager for the Northwest nine states. A short nine months later, he and Leslie had celebrated the birth of their first-born child, little six-pound-two-ounce Lisa. Lisa was a bald headed bouncing baby full of energy and enthusiasm. Edward's little family now lived in a much nicer, much larger two-bedroom house near the city.

Several months went by. Lisa grew into a toddler and sprouted her first fuzzy black hairs. Edward was spending a lot of time at work. He traveled from one store to another sometimes by car and sometimes by air. He traveled with a briefcase crammed full of monotonous paperwork and he often went with less food and rest than he needed. When he did eat, he ate at late night diners and in the stores simple cafeterias. When he had free time he spent it with Leslie and Lisa and they were always on his mind no matter where Edward was or what he was doing. It was all for them.

Edward had returned home from working a complete remodel on an old storefront recently acquired by McKnight. Now his travel bag lay abandoned on the newly brown shag carpeted floor and Leslie stood just inside the kitchen playing with little Lisa. Edward's coat – Lee's coat, hung carelessly on the back of a cheap dining room chair. Edward took the child from Leslie and Lisa started crying.

He looked down at the most precious face in the world to him and realized that the baby was crying because to her he was a stranger. In the mind of an eighteen month old, the eight weeks he had been gone was forever. Leslie took the baby and her crying subsided and Edward stood there a moment, head down and in awe of the circumstances. Then a new looking old style black telephone still equipped with an old fashioned dial and made of metal began to ring.

Almost without thinking Edward picked up the handset and whispered a tired "hello". He recognized the voice of Mr. Nathan Cantrell – the Northwest regional manager of Mc Knight Stores. Edward had been with his family for less than an hour and his boss was already looking for him. Mr. Cantrell told Edward to be in Los Angeles by nine o'clock Monday morning. It was now eight o'clock Saturday night and Edward had just arrived back in Portland, Oregon. In frustration, Edward turned to explain to his young wife that he had to leave again early Monday morning. Almost as if little Lisa understood what this meant, she started to cry again.

Things shifted and Edward found himself on the airplane. He replayed in his mind how he had earned his position as District manager and quickly come to be both Mr. Young's boss and Mr. Melvin's boss. Now Edward sat with his head relaxed against an airline pillow. He was thinking of Leslie and Lisa and remembering the leisurely Sunday that they had spent together. He wished he could be with his family, but he knew he had to work until Friday or Saturday at the earliest. He took a deep breath, closed his eyes and fell into a peaceful slumber.

Edward did not see the bright orange flash that eerily lighted the plane. He did not hear the sickening scraping sound of the misguided small airplane that had misread its instrument panel and wandered into the side of the airliner. He felt no pain and had no time to feel panic. Something in his mind had just begun to sound to an alarm – and then there was nothing. Nothing except the strange feeling that instead of going down as one might expect in an airline crash – Edward felt he was going up. Edward breathed deeply once more and this time it was his last breath. Both planes crashed into an uninhabited and sparsely treed wasteland. There was an investigation and a search for someone or something to blame. Tears were shed by family members and loved ones and after awhile, as it always does, life on Earth marched on. Lee's book went blank.

Chapter 13

Lee placed the book back on one of the shelves. It didn't belong on that shelf and the book simply moved itself to the correct place. Nathaniel appeared in the room.

"I think I understand some of the lessons I was learning in that life but maybe you could help me understand a few more," Lee said.

"What do you feel you understand?" Nathaniel asked.

"Well, I understand the obvious lesson about the value of honesty that Edward learned when he learned he could be trusted to handle other people's money. But what other lessons were there?" Lee asked.

"One of the lessons Edward may have learned is how it feels to be treated by someone that views themselves as so superior that they need not even acknowledge another," Nathaniel said.

Lee nodded. "Yes, and maybe also that even the so-called bum wanted to be treated with respect and get what is advertised."

Nathaniel nodded.

"Edward also must have learned what it is like to be away from his family because he was trying to support them. He may have learned what it is like for your own child to not even recognize you because you are gone so much," Nathaniel said.

"Maybe he also learned how to go from being the newest hire to being the boss and all of the things that go along with that," Lee said.

"Yes, and obviously he learned what it is to experience death in an airline crash and to leave behind the beloved family he was doing his best to support," Nathaniel said.

Lee nodded his head and changed the topic.

"Can you tell me why the books are arranged as they are on the shelves?" Lee asked.

"Time does not exist here at Home. The books are arranged in a more or less loose fashion because of this fact. It is possible for a soul to move between lives in any order. They could return to any life or Visit they have ever experienced at any point within that Visit. A soul could even decide to return to a life that had originally ended early for some reason and live on beyond that point," Nathaniel said.

"Once when I was a boy I was in an accident and was miraculously uninjured. Do you mean that I might have once left Earth in that accident, and returned to Earth and I now remember that I was uninjured?" Lee asked.

"That is possible," Nathaniel said gesturing. "The answer is here in these books."

"So, what is reality?" Lee asked.

"Reality is that which is perceived to be real by a soul. When you add action, intent, and design to a perception it is molded into reality," Nathaniel said.

"Do some objects exist, or are they all just perceived?" Lee asked.

"An object is the result of a perceived reality that has been acted upon, intended, and designed by a soul to accomplish a task or fulfill a perceived desire. No 'thing' is truly solid. All things are made up of molecules, which contain as much or more space than material. Part of the reason that objects eventually wear out is that the perception, intent and actions that mold an object into existence begin to fade. The fading allows more space within the molecules of the object and reduces the strength of perception, intention and action that originally molded the object together to a perceived solid state. Even our bodies are not solid they are a combination of space, matter and the planning, perception and intention – together referred to as action that brought them to life," Nathaniel said.

"Do our parents have anything to do with the formation of our bodies?" Lee asked.

"Yes, that is one way to perceive it. Since action formed our bodies initially, it could seem that the actions of our parents were the catalyst of the creation of our bodies. However, we must step outside our perceptions of reality and understand that our bodies are not formed without our involvement. Our involvement takes place in the City of Choices and the City of Planning and is based on actions intended within a given purpose wheel."

"Is it possible for people on Earth to communicate with people here?"

"Most things are possible. But, during your recent Visit to Earth, did you ever attempt to speak with someone that did not understand your language, and whose language you did not understand?" Nathaniel asked.

"Yes."

"Then you recall the difficulty that you had communicating in that type of situation. It is very similar here when we attempt to communicate to Visitors that are not within our target age ranges. Our language here is a thought language. Therefore, some thoughts modify the meaning or intention of other thoughts to create realities, events or concepts. Just as in the languages of the Earth some words modify the meaning of other words to better explain perceptions, things, events or concepts," Nathaniel said.

"I am not sure I understood all of that but let's move on. Does the personality of a Soul die when that Soul leaves Earth?"

"The personality is an outward representation of the nature of the soul that inhabits the body. While personality can be affected by experience and circumstances, the soul chooses all of their circumstances and experiences. Therefore a soul's personality is only altered when the soul chooses to alter her or his personality's attributes. Each personality is retained in its entirety here in the Hall of Review and each can help us learn from our Visits."

"Why are some people on Earth rich and some poor?" Lee asked.

"Everything that exists on Earth and many things that exist in this portion of the Other Side has at least two sides. If the concept of rich exists then the concept of poor is its opposite or other side. If the concept of health exists then the concept of sickness is its other side. If the concept of happiness exists then the concept of sadness is its other side. Each emotion has an 'other' side; happiness is the other side of sadness, love is the other side of hate, fear is the other side of bravery and anger is the other side of joy. If a person believes he or she is experiencing a certain emotion than he or she *is* experiencing it. If you believe that you are experiencing love, than you *are* experiencing love. You have chosen to experience love. No one has *made* you love them. You have chosen to experience the emotion of love. No one has ever made you angry. You have chosen to experience anger. No one has ever made you happy. You have chosen to experience happiness," Nathaniel said.

"But it seems like sometimes people made me happy or angry by doing certain things. What about that?"

"These people did things that you judged in one way or another. You chose to experience happiness or anger that the person did a particular thing or acted in a particular manner. The same is true when you judged certain things that happened to you as good, or great. You could have chosen to experience anger, frustration, or even expectation at the same exact actions of others. If you look back on your most recent Visit carefully, you will note that when a certain thing happened one time you may have felt extreme happiness and when the same thing happened again you may have felt only mild happiness. It could continue to the point where you have experienced a certain thing so many times that experiencing it again now brings only disappointment."

Lee considered all of this and slowly began nodding.

"This is the nature of Earth and the nature of this portion of the World Beyond. Each contains a construct where all that is – is reflected in at least two variations. On

Earth we refer to the two variations as opposites. Here we sometimes refer to them as others," Nathaniel said.

Where do Souls come from?" Lee asked.

"Souls exist. They do not come from or go anywhere," Nathaniel answered.

"How are we supposed to find out whom we are and what our purpose is while we are on Earth?"

"You may find out by doing that which they have purposed to do."

"How do you know what you purposed to do?" Lee asked.

"Look within yourself and around yourself and pay attention to the so-called coincidences that are happening to you."

"What if I've looked within myself and around myself and I can't figure out my purpose?"

"Then ask yourself to reveal your purpose or ask God about your purpose wheel. Ask your friends and your family and look deeper within yourself and see," Nathaniel said.

Seth and I moved on toward the City of Planning. We had each already left one of ourselves to wait for Lee at the City of Choices and I knew that Lee would soon conclude his questions and begin to make his choices.

Chapter 14

Seth and I approached a shining small city that was apparently built on a cloud. The cloud seemed to be everywhere one might expect to see grass or sidewalks or streets. It seemed to be everywhere one might expect to see sky and water as well. There was apparently no need for vehicles of any kind because souls were moving and transporting by thought from one part of the city to another.

If I had seen this city on Earth I would have been certain that I was dreaming. The City of Planning floated in midair and bobbed gently as if the wind were blowing. Yet it seemed as if we were inside rather than outside and I felt no wind. Above the city there was what appeared to be a large office building with hundreds of shining glass-like windows. It was lying on its side rather than standing erect as it would have on Earth and yet it looked perfectly natural that way. I was certain that the building had not fallen over but rather been constructed and designed to be on its side. The building was floating in a sea of white billowing clouds and rocked gently as if nestled in the arms of a caring mother.

Above the large floating office building I saw the outline of a huge brass and gold colored door. An old fashioned looking silver sparkling skeleton key hung from the door knob and an impressive looking fifteen-foot angel complete with ten-foot long, five-foot wide sword stood guarding the door. The angel was garbed in a white tunic similar to the one I had found myself in at the Library. I had the feeling no one entered that door unless whoever or whatever was behind it specifically invited them.

Nearer the 'ground'; if you can call the lower part of the cloud the ground, souls were moving inside and outside of another large multidimensional building. The building was like nothing I had ever seen and I understood only that it was some type of structure and not what its purpose might be. It had appendages all around it and through it in every conceivable direction and in some directions that did not seem conceivable. It had 'doorways' and 'windows' or at least I thought those strange things reminded me of doorways and windows. They were of a shape I had never seen on Earth and I did not know the name of the shape. The building was neither standing erect nor lying on its side but rather floating and changing its orientation as I watched.

Many souls stood or floated or levitated around the building in a kind of air ballet. Each Soul had an energy field in a glowing group of colors surrounding it and the energy fields shifted and the colors changed as souls exchanged thoughts and plans with other souls. Here, like the City of Choices, everything seemed to be fully visible no matter from what vantage point the object or Soul was viewed. If there were offices in this building, and if there were souls 'working' in those offices, and if those souls had framed photographs on their desks, then those souls could see not only the front and the top and bottom of the frame but all sides of the frame – all without moving the frame or shifting their perspective. Yet it would be more than that. It would be as if everything in the photograph could move, change sizes, change positions and simultaneously remain in precisely the same place, size and position. It would be as each item in the picture could be viewed from all directions. It was both strange and wonderful to begin to understand the nature of multidimensionality.

The City of Planning seemed more like a busy rural area than a city. Fields of hundreds of acres of apparent clouds seemed to produce fruits, vegetables and other plants such as I had never seen on Earth. Planners floated above the clouds at all levels. They hovered above and below ground level and passed through ground level glowing in a glorious variety of ever changing colors. These beings, represented in what looked to me to be typical Earth style farmer attire, worked in a way that I did not understand. Some made strange movements with their hands and plants and other unusual things began to grow. Others simply looked in a particular direction and growth began, changed or stopped. One Planter moved her head slightly to one direction and a three dimensional building appeared from nowhere and from nothing. Another looked toward an Earth river and a bridge appeared.

Above the Planners one being stood wearing a suit of multicolored glass. It floated in every direction simultaneously and occasional blue, white and silver explosions of light and music burst from the being. Its eyes were a blazing gold and it shone in brilliant light. It was dressed in a gold colored tunic. It was neither male nor female, neither short nor tall. It simply moved and changed – maybe rotated is a better term - from one appearance to another. Its hair was a rainbow of colors mixed with colors I knew no name for and yet it looked natural and not artificially colored.

"Do you understand what you are seeing?" Seth asked.

I admitted that I did not.

"The planners are planning for what Earth will call future events," Seth said.

It made sense to me. The Planters planned Earth Visits and when those visits included changes in structures on Earth, they planned that as well. "What is that thing above the Planners?" I asked.

"That is a Designer. I don't fully understand their purpose yet myself," Seth answered.

I marveled for a while at the Designer and I wondered how many other beings existed that I had never seen or considered. And then things shifted and I found myself back at the City of Choices.

Lee was moving towards me. His face glowed in the truths of what he had remembered at the Hall of Records. Joy and knowledge leapt from his countenance and lifted my own spirit. Seth was standing in the same place and wearing the same clothing as when I had originally encountered him here.

Lee came to me and we embraced and it was as if we had never been apart. Then Lee and Seth embraced.

"Seth, I owe you an apology," Lee started but Seth interrupted him.

"Don't be so hard on yourself Dad. Everything happened just as we planned," Seth said smiling.

Lee looked toward me and cocked his head. I smiled and nodded. It had of course been the plan for Seth to leave Earth at the bus accident.

"The planners suggested that you learn to lose a son to death just as you had earlier learned to lose the trust of a child that did not recognize you because you were constantly working. I volunteered to be that son. Now, you and mom go on and do the things that are in your plan for here. When we have all finished, I'll meet you both at the City of Planning," Seth said.

Lee smiled and nodded and hugged Seth again. Seth gave me a hug and a kiss on the cheek then he disappeared.

Lee and I kissed and it was the sweetest kiss I could recall from any lifetime. Our spirits merged and it was the most intimate moment of all. It was a moment beyond explanation, a moment far beyond the most intense pleasure ever possible on Earth. We joined together not *as* one – but truly one. We became two sides of the same coin, two views of the same structure, two hearts locked together and intertwined in love. Inexplicable joy filled our unified spirit. Unfathomable love surged from our unified soul. It was a love without a thought of self and without a hint of being separate. We did not pull apart because now, for us, there was no apart. We simply were together. We traveled together through the City of Choices, the Body Mall and on into the City of Planning.

While we were entering the City of Planning things again shifted and we found ourselves in the Hall of Review watching Sara as she opened her first twinkling book. We did not need to stay to review her incarnations because we had both sent one of ourselves to review her lives when we first left the Library. Instead we moved to the point where Sara would ask her questions so that we might share that experience with her. We kept ourselves in a dimension that Sara could not yet comprehend so that we would not disturb her as she accomplished this needed review process.

Keiko was the relative from a distant incarnation that answered Sara's questions.

"Do things exist on a physical plane or a spiritual plane?" Sara asked.

"Both the physical and the spiritual are misconceptions because neither exists absolutely. That which seems on the physical plane is an observation, which is limited by the five senses employed on that plane. Not only are the five senses incapable of sensing that which is beyond the senses, but each sense is also incomplete in itself. For example, there are things that cross your plane of vision that you do not see. Sometimes you do not see these things because you are not paying attention to them and other times you do not see these things because they cannot be represented visually. Wind is one such thing that cannot be represented visually. One can see the effects of wind, but not the wind itself," Keiko answered.

"What is it about the spiritual that is a misconception?"

"On Earth we try to understand the spiritual in physical terms. That would be like trying to understand the desert using only the terminology of the sea. The thought picture you paint is incomplete and misleading, therefore, it is a misconception of that which is."

"How can the spiritual be understood if not on physical terms?" Sara asked.

"It must be understood as that which is beyond the physical. That which is beyond time, beyond the three dimensional planet, and beyond human thought."

"Can you define the spiritual for me?" Sara asked.

"The spiritual is and always shall be as it is."

Sara looked perplexed but pushed forward in her questioning. "What is the purpose of life on Earth?"

"To live, learn, observe, and experience, within a selected time frame, the effects and truths of various activities, ideas, actions and motions and how those truths shift and change."

"Alright," Sara said. "What is the purpose of the World Beyond?"

"To review, choose and plan more effects and truths of various activities, ideas, actions and motions outside of a time frame and to serve as a link between Earth and Home."

"Is there anything beyond the Other Side?" Sara asked.

"That which is eternal or that which does not change or move. Beyond the Other Side is that which has become and now is forevermore."

"What is the purpose of humankind beyond Home?" Sara asked.

"Humankind's purpose is to be simultaneously temporal and eternal. It is to be the sum of what humankind has become," Keiko said.

"What is it like beyond the Other Side?"

"It is like static. There is no Earthly thing and no Earthly activity. All that is – is – without change," Keiko said.

"Wow. It seems like it would be boring," Sara said.

"Not many humans can easily value eternal rest or eternity without change or motion because humankind was designed to experience a variety of Visits and tasks. That is why many choose to travel between the various realms of existence. Some humans can move on to become Planners but I think that is about as far as most care to go. Other beings exist which were designed to interact within the eternal realm."

"But, isn't the goal to be at the ultimate or the final place?" Sara asked.

"Why do you believe that there must be a single ultimate or final place?"

Sara was not certain why she believed that.

"I guess that it was just how I thought it worked," Sara said.

"Do you judge one goal or design superior to another?"

"So, you are saying that no matter if I choose to be on Earth, on some other planet, here, or beyond, that each is equal to the other?"

"Perhaps not equal since that term implies mathematical connotations. But each is of value," Keiko said.

"Tell me more about Home," Sara requested.

"Home is that which it is perceived to be by the one who perceives it."

"Are you saying I cannot describe it to anyone because it is different for everyone?" Sara asked.

"You may describe what it is like to you. This may be of value to others even though they may perceive it differently when there turn comes to experience it," Keiko said.

"If I were on Earth could you show me the World Beyond?"

"A better question would be is an Earth resident willing to see it."

"And if they are?" Sara asked.

"Then allow them to open their eyes and look around," Keiko said.

"Wouldn't they just see Earth?"

"They would need to stop looking at things."

"Stop looking at things?" Sara asked.

"They would need to start looking at the space between things. One method of doing that would be to look up."

"Wouldn't they just see birds and airplanes, tall buildings, clouds and sky?"

"If they looked only at the space between the birds and other things, then what would they see?" Keiko asked.

"The sky?" Sara asked.

"And what would they see beyond the sky?"

"They cannot see beyond the sky with their physical eyes," Sara said.

"Did I suggest that they use their 'physical' eyes?"

"How can they use other than their physical eyes?" Sara asked.

"They must open their soul and see with it." Keiko said.

"And what would they see?"

"They would see that on Earth there is no end to change and that at Home there is no change to end."

Lee and I moved forward within the dimension that Sara could not comprehend and tended a question of our own to Keiko.

"What about those who subscribe to a particular religion?" We asked.

"Each Soul is free to choose to embrace any religion or no religion at all," Keiko said simply.

"We understand that a soul may choose to incarnate as an Element. Can you tell us more about that?" We asked.

"A soul is not limited in its choices of incarnations or tasks. There are no limits to what a soul may choose. They are able to do anything, become anything and endure anything. A soul may choose any set of purposes, any goal, and any objective. One such objective is to incarnate as an Element," Keiko said.

"What is an Element?" We asked.

"A few of the Earth elements include weather, light, time, plague, fire, disease and all of their other sides," Keiko said.

Chapter 15

Lee and I traveled back toward the Library and found Allen standing nearby.

"Thank you, Leena. You were a great help to me," Allen said.

"How could have I been a help to you?" I asked.

"When you died I really began to look at my life. I turned myself around and made something of myself. I had to because I was alive and you were gone and it didn't seem right."

I hugged Allen. "I am no more valuable than you are. We are each uniquely valuable."

Then, I did something I could never have imagined myself doing. I told Allen about Noah's wheels of life and Joan's clocks and Ferris wheels. I explained them carefully, and patiently answered his questions. Allen asked many of the same questions of me that I had asked and it seemed both strange and wonderful to have transformed from student to teacher. I realized that we are all part student and part teacher. We all question and we each have knowledge and experiences which can answer the questions of others. When Allen asked a question I did not know the answer to, the truth of the matter came to me from an internal voice that I instinctively trusted and I spoke it confidently. I must have seemed as advanced to Allen as Noah, Joan and Grandma had seemed to me.

I stood speaking with Allen and simultaneously moved on with Lee back to the Library.

An angel appeared. Her shoulder length blond hair fell in a wave of curls over her delicate face and accented her gently tilted woman-child's head. Her wings were plush and feathery and her back was surrounded by a gentle petite curve of wing. Her white tunic fell in pleats from its plunging scoop neckline into long loose sleeves and ended at her tiny bare feet. Soft clouds of white and billowing clouds of a thousand shades of blue surrounded her. She extended her hand, her index finger outstretched and a dove suddenly appeared a few inches above her hand. Its wings were unfolded and it flared its feet as it came in for an easy landing. She lifted the bird and it sang a lovely song to her as she nodded in understanding. She turned to Lee and me smiling.

"The Master has requested a meeting with you," she said.

We shrugged and nodded to the angel.

In an instant we were transported to the City of Planning and I remembered seeing the huge brass and gold colored door the first time I had been here. This time we stood above the city and looked down on it. We stood as if on solid ground in the middle of the air far above the city and far above the office building that still lay floating on its side. The angel standing at the door snapped to a position of attention at the sight of us and then relaxed as he saw the tiny beautiful angel that accompanied us. He moved his sword across his chest as if in salute and stood to one side.

The lock behind him dissolved and the door opened without assistance. When the door first opened we could see nothing but a field of billowing white clouds. Then slowly, as we stepped through the doors opening the view changed. Now we seemed to be standing on a landing looking into an eternity of tiny stars the size the head of a pin and several slightly out of focus planetary size lights clustered in a loose circular shape. The landing beneath us shuddered and the angel released the dove she had been holding. The dove flew out into the majestic blue ethereal lights and the landing beneath our feet seemed to hasten to follow her.

We moved onward in this fashion for a while and then the starry scene began to fade and a field of resplendently colored unique plants came into view. A multidimensional green cactus like plant danced in the foreground. It moved in a delicate almost dainty dance of delight and we smiled at the sight of it. Pillars of red, green and gold stood nestled like bushy trees just behind the cactus and seemed to sway with the same rhythm. We looked further into the scene and noticed what appeared to be an opening of a cave rounded and carved into a sky like pattern behind and above the plants. The cave seemed to rotate slowly moving left to right in a gentle circular motion but also moving up and down as if bouncing from the ground. We moved into the opening of the cave and the view changed once again.

A roman style group of pillars stood before us and a group of white robed angels played shiny long trumpets. The sound was unique in its beauty, simplicity and majesty. Above and behind the trumpet-playing angels stood a group of beings robed in silver, gold and royal blue. The assembly was countless and they seemed to continue moving into and across the scene before us. Then, as if on cue the thousands of beings split their formation exactly in the center and moved in military precision so that another door could be seen. This door was ten thousand feet tall and made of every precious stone we had ever seen and many we had never seen before. The door burst open and a light so bright that we momentarily thought we had been blinded shone from it. An orchestra of thousands upon thousands floated through the door playing a regal march. Each musician was dressed in white and each carried a gold, silver or royal blue instrument. It was the sound of a thousand symphonies playing together and yet more than that, it was the sound of joy, the sound of peace and the sound of honor.

A thousand angels each larger than the one before came through the door until the last two angels entered single file and had to stoop to enter through the door. Another burst of light shone forth from the door and a choir of a thousand angels began singing in unison. Their song was the most beautiful sound and with it they seemed to announce that the Master was nearby.

And then, it happened. A being dressed in a beautiful gold robe and wearing a beautiful gold ring on its hand walked in and every angel fell to their knees. The being lifted its hand and motioned them all to rise. Her/his face was like the brightest star and I could not look at her/him face to face. His/her arms and legs were like the strongest iron and he/she seemed to simultaneously burn, glow and shine.

The being just stood there for a moment in all its glory and we were amazed at the sight. Then in a flash of light, it disappeared. In its place stood an ordinary looking man dressed in simple white overalls and simple white boots. He made a dismissive gesture with one hand and the thousands of angels, choirs and orchestras disappeared. The man simply walked towards us his hands outstretched.

"Leena, Lee, won't you please come in," the man said pleasantly.

I glanced at Lee but he seemed as confused as I was. I knew that we were both wondering just who this man was and what the glorious procession we had just viewed was all about.

"I must apologize," the man said smiling.

Lee and I exchanged glances again.

"My people sometimes get a bit carried away when introducing me. I think they enjoy the pomp and piety too much. They sure do enjoy putting on a show," he said.

A table appeared and a feast fit for a thousand kings was upon it. We had not even thought about food since we had been here and even though it looked delicious, we realized that we were not in the least bit hungry. The man waved a hand and the feast disappeared.

"I hope you don't mind, I'm sending that to some Visitors that really need it. We certainly have no need for it here."

Lee and I smiled.

"You must be wondering why I asked you here," he said.

Lee and I nodded simultaneously.

"I have a favor to ask of you. You are both involved to a degree but it is primarily you, Lee, that must decide whether to grant me this favor or not," the man said.

"Sir, may I ask who you are?" Lee asked.

"Like you, I am essentially Soul and Spirit. It is just that I have a rather prestigious title. It's all really a bit much sometimes what with all these beings fawning over me constantly," the man said.

"Sir, may I ask your title?" Lee asked even more quietly and reverently.

"I shall not bore you with the countless titles and names I have been given by mankind. Please know me simply as the Great I Am," he said.

Lee and I both gasped.

"Oh, please. Relax!" The Great I Am said.

Lee and I tried to smile.

"Lee, I would that you were willing to do a special task for me in your next Visit. Leena, I would that you allow me to multiply your gift a thousand fold that you may assist Lee with his task," The Great I Am said.

"What may I do for you my Lord?" Lee asked bowing.

"Please, please. Just relax, be yourself. All I've ever wanted was to be known by souls and to commune with them as they commune with me," the Great I Am said.

"I would be pleased to do your bidding," Lee said.

"Earth has become a place that needs much assistance. People are running here and there in a hurry to accomplish nothing. They war among themselves serving the masters of money and power but their masters have neither. For Earthly power and possession, and all the things of Earth are within the realm of that which is temporary. No person may truly own any thing nor may any thing own any person. Things are not as they seem. Material things are of so little importance in the scheme of all that is. You, Lee shall be one who knows the truth and tells the truth freely. Men and women shall not accept you easily just as they have never accepted anyone sent by me or by my father. But, you shall go and be my emissary. You shall know the difference between what is and what shall be and you shall give men a glimpse of hope and dash of love by planting into their hearts the truth of what is important. Leena you shall give them the song of life and they shall rejoice in hearing it. Mankind shall bring you great Earthly wealth and you shall give the wealth to those who are in need. You shall need nothing for I grant you the blessing of plenty without the burden of greed. Lee, you shall have the power to see people for who they truly are and you shall share with those who are willing their unique purpose and mission. You shall point them in the right direction and I shall lead them to find their core purpose and prepare them for what must now come to pass. For in the days of your life there shall be a great uprising of a small power that is currently considered insignificant. The children shall arise and sing songs of joy with hearts filled with love and the children shall lead those who are old in body to the truth of eternal youth of spirit. Will you do this for me?" the Great I Am asked.

"I shall give my best to accomplish this task," Lee said.

"I shall support him in all he does," I said.

"Lee, I give you the gifts of sight and second sight and I give you the gifts of hearing and second hearing. I give you the gifts of knowledge and understanding and I give you the gift of healing and cleansing. I give you the gift of love and the gift of plenty and I send you an invisible invincible angel that shall be your guard and another that shall be your constant contact with me and my kingdom that whatsoever you ask in the context of your mission shall be provided to you. Leena, I give you the amplified gift of song. People shall wonder at the power within your voice and you will tell them that it is all in you," the Great I Am said.

The Great I Am stood and walked back through the thousand foot tall door and our tiny angel appeared and led us back to where we were. I knew that upon my first public appearance as a singer I would point to the audience and say; "It's all in you!" The words would be my message of thanks to those I had been given to bless with song and my words of encouragement to all who heard. I wanted them all to know that all that is, truly is in all of us.

I took Lee's hand and together we embraced. It was the season for our next mission.

Chapter 16

We finally felt that we understood. The truth is that all the mysteries of life are not really mysteries at all. Nothing happens coincidently. It is all planned. All of the life's lessons are planned. Every *good* thing that happens is planned for a reason and the same is true for every *bad* thing that happens. Nothing can ever harm the spirit being that resides within the human body. We are everlasting until we are eternal and we are eternal until we are everlasting. We are not our bodies and our bodies are not us. We are soul and spirit but we are more than just soul and spirit. We think and we learn and we realize. We are that which experiences and we are that which chooses experience. There is no sickness that transcends Earth. There is no death that passes Earth's cloudy gates.

Time is a tool, not to be sold or traded, but to be given to a task of choice, a purpose of choice or a plan of choice. The Great I Am blesses us. We do the work of the Master and the work we do is a part of our plan, our purpose and our reason for existence. We are a part of all that is, with no judgment of comparison to the other parts of what is. We are neither better nor worse than anyone else. We are the same and yet different, a part of the whole, yet whole within ourselves.

The Source is the cause of all that is and we are a part of the Source. We do not control the Source and the Source does not control us. We do not judge the Source and the Source does not judge us. We work together, separate wheels turning together for a common purpose within a multidimensional wheel. Without the Source, we would have no power and without humankind, the Source would have no purpose. We are an essential part of the Source, a part of God. The universe would not work properly without the tasks we are designed to accomplish and the same is true of every person who has ever lived or shall ever live.

We are part planner and part of that which experiences the plan. We are timeless, either within or outside of a time frame. We are beyond the limit of dimensions, either within or outside of the three dimensional planets. We are all that we are even when we are not aware of all that we are. We are more than we ever believed ourselves to be and yet we are who we have been designed to be by the power of the Source.

There is no success and there is no failure. Both success and failure, like good and bad, are judgments of our own and the expressed judgments of others. One of our great purposes is to learn, another is to experience and yet another is to assist others in learning and experiencing.

Lee and I willingly lay down judgments of all kinds. We will not judge success and failure, good or bad, happy or sad, rich or poor, black or white. We will not judge young or old, gifted or challenged, male or female. We will not judge those who choose to view life as something other than we see it, we will not judge others, nor will we judge ourselves. We will simply be as we are and allow others to be as they are.

We know that anything that any person believes and desires is possible in life. Not only is it possible, but by the simple active belief and desire of it, it is written into the person's path of travel. If possibility is absent in this Visit, than it will be present in the next Visit, or the one after that. There is no waiting because everything happens simultaneously. This life, next life, the one before and the one after are all present in each rising of the sun, each breaking of a wave, each sighting of a songbird in flight.

There is no lack of time, for there is no time. There is no lack of anything, because anything can easily be created by a soul and brought into existence. The truth is there are no limits and that active belief, is yet another of the elements of the power of the Source.

Now that we understand, we are ready to conclude the planning for our next Visit. We take on our tasks with the energy and the desire that comes from knowing that no other beings in all of creation could ever perform our tasks just as no one other than you can perform your tasks. We are ready.

Lee and I go together because we have asked that it be so. We left the Library and transported ourselves back to the City of Planning. When we arrived everyone was here together in a huge room that reminded us of an enormous family room we had once seen. We saw Seth, Sara, Danny, Marie, Macy, Doreen, Noah, Keiko, Nathaniel, Rick, Steven Pritchard, my mother Lynn and my father Roy. Spirit Guides for each Soul were also present. We had all decided to Visit Earth again and expand upon the lessons that we had all reviewed. Some of us needed to complete tasks we had neglected to complete on a previous Visit, including myself. Others simply wanted to learn more about love and about life from an Earth perspective. Yet others were here simply to assist those of us that needed and desired assistance. We all knew that portions of our Visit would seem painful in the moments that we experienced them. We understood that there would be times during our Visit that we would judge events and deeds as good and bad. We all knew that no matter what happened on Earth, we were safe, loved and valued by everyone at Home and by ourselves.

I had loved the area of Earth called Hawaii and had only been able to travel there once in my life as Leena. I suggested that we all live in Hawaii on the next Visit and everyone agreed. Lee and I would be husband and wife on our next Visit since we were now soul mates.

"Let's meet on the beach when we are seven years old," I suggested.

"OK, you be six, I'll be seven," Lee said.

"We'll grow up best friends and then get married in our early twenties," I suggested.

Seth and Sara decided to be husband and wife and have two children. I agreed to be Seth and Sara's oldest daughter.

Danny and Marie Boyce would also be husband and wife and Lee agreed to be their oldest son.

"We should have a dog for our children," suggested Seth.

"Good idea," agreed Sara.

"Hay, I've never been a dog! I can learn to be constantly happy, always giving and never expect anything but a few moments of attention in return," Lynn said excitedly.

I heard a barking sound and turned to see Wally. He transformed before my eyes from a dog into a nice looking light-haired man in his mid thirties. "I'd like to try a Visit as a human," Wally said.

"Great idea!" Lee and I said in unison.

"Wally, you can be my next door neighbor," I suggested. Wally agreed.

"I have agreed to perform a purpose task. All I can say of my task is that it somehow involves a tree near the ocean," David said.

"OK," said Seth. "The Planners have suggested that we learn how to suffer the loss of one of our children."

"The Planners have also suggested that since I was a minister in my last visit, I be a criminal in the next. I could be the man that murders the child you are losing," Rick suggested.

"Alright," agreed Sara. "Would any one like to be the child?"

Doreen smiled.

"Well, I never really wanted to go back to the Earth for an entire life. This way I could go back for a short life and still learn how to die as a child. Could it happen when I'm ten years old?" Doreen asked.

"Great!" They all agreed.

"I'll be your best friend, Lee," Nathaniel volunteered.

"And I'll be yours, Leena," Keiko said.

And on and on the planning went.

Noah volunteered to be the favorite teacher of Lee and Leena. Macy agreed to be Leena's voice instructor and assist her in preparing for a singing career. Roy volunteered to be the commanding officer for Seth in his role. Steven agreed to come into the Visit at an opportune moment and be of assistance to Leena. With the plan nearly finished, we went our separate ways to finish our work. The Planners would put together all the final touches and we would each review every element of our Visit to be certain that we were happy with our choices.

One by one, each of us began to prepare to leave Home and Visit Earth. Each of us would send a part of ourselves into our physical mother at the moment of conception. The remainder of ourselves would remain at Home until the moment of birth and then every part of ourselves would be sent into our new body at the moment we drew our first breath. A Planner and a Designer would travel with each of us into our future body at the moment of conception. They would travel in Essential Form or EF for short, meaning they would travel without a physical body.

Planners plan and Designers design all of the elements that we had chosen at the Body Mall. The Planner and Designer complete their task of making certain that all of the elements we had chosen would grow into reality. They usually leave at a point in our body's development known as quickening. Sometimes, for some reason I do not yet understand, Planners and Designers leave before their work on the new body is complete. We know this happens, because we see the results in anomalies of children with a variety of challenging conditions. Is their plan to leave early? I do not know.

When the Planner and Designer leave, the Spirit Guide and more of the soul arrives. Once the first breath had been inhaled and expelled the soul will be encased within the body for the duration of this Visit and the Spirit Guide would remain with them continually.

I understood that the movement of Essential Forms on Earth had resulted in people photographing orbs of light that some thought to be the image of a ghost. The truth was more simple. Some EF beings are mischievous and they seek out people who easily believe in ghosts and the like to tease them. Planners have a duel essence, one side being a bodily representation and the other being EF. They can exhibit a see-through body on Earth, but they are not as good at that as they are at creating orbs of light. Designers are better at creating a visible ghost-like body and they excel at producing a variety of chilling literally unearthly sounds. Since Planners and Designers exist in reality, they unintentionally leave some visible clues to their existence. This is a Source level directive and as such is not changeable, so Planners and Designers have found a way to have fun with the reality they cannot change. They exist primarily in EF and only choose to materialize in body form to communicate, or to tease lower level beings. This explains most of the so-called real life ghost stories.

There was a grand party and we all joined together in a happy celebration. We were each going to Earth to gain more experience and knowledge. We all knew that once we arrived back at Earth we would not remember the planning sessions or what we did here. But, even without their memory, our choices would be brought to us again and again by the Planners and hopefully we would make the choice to carry out our planned tasks. Each of the group that had chosen to spend our next Visit together began to leave. First Danny and Marie, Seth and Sara, Noah, Keiko, Roy, Steven, Macy and Rick left. Then Nathaniel and Lee and I prepared to go.

Our Earthly bodies were ready and we gathered all of who we are from the wide expanse of the World Beyond and sent ourselves into tiny incomplete and seemingly helpless infant bodies. Joan whispered encouraging words to me as my tiny body grew. Seemingly, a moment later I saw a dark tunnel and a very bright light at the end of the tunnel. This time I seemed to move down the tunnel and my movement was more gradual and more difficult. This time I moved little by little down the tunnel-fighting inch after inch in a tight squeeze. My body emerged and I took my first breath. All that I am came to rest inside of a tiny baby's body. Joan stood beside me and comforted me.

I found myself naked and cold in a hospital room. I looked around and for just a moment I remembered everything. My body was tiny but my mind was complete in the knowledge of all that I am and all that I have been and all that I shall be. I was born. I heard my Earth father Seth yelp with glee.

"Oh, she is beautiful! I'll remember today, December 2, 2019 all of my life! Let's name her Leann!" Seth said enthusiastically.

"We have to give her a Hawaiian middle name," Sara said.

They spoke more words, but in that moment my memory of my previous life and my life in the World Beyond began to fade and I felt the vale of human thought begin to form. I began to cry. I cried and cried. I had lost my memory of who I had been and at that moment I did not know that I would ever regain it. I cried tears of loss.

Now I only knew that I was cold and hungry. I heard a gentle voice saying words I did not understand and I felt a gentle rocking and a gentle kiss and I began to relax.

I am loved!

Paul L. Bailey

Part 2

Chapter 17

Thursday, February 6, 2025

Lieutenant Colonel Seth Woodson stepped from the olive drab Jeep and returned the salute of Senior Airman Peter Canon. The Airman steered the jeep back onto the narrow roadway and hurried away. The Lieutenant Colonel was in full dress uniform and dozens of medals sparkled from the front of his uniform. He stood tall and his masculine physique was apparent in the confines of his tightly fitting uniform. He removed his officer's hat and his short sandy blond hair ruffled in the evening breeze.

The Lieutenant Colonel's military housing was plain and simple. It was a white and grey condominium and the Lieutenant Colonel and his family lived in a two-bedroom apartment on the main floor. Seth walked through the door and called to his family.

"Sara, Kiki – I'm here!" he said.

A beautiful young dark haired woman with dazzling gray eyes and a suave sexy smile came around the corner. She was dressed in white shorts and a white blouse and with her tan skin and the glow of love and happiness that surrounded her she took Seth's breath away. Six-year-old Leann Liakiki Woodson, who answered to 'Kiki' for short, followed Sara. Kiki's red hair and freckles had been the source of countless jokes between Seth and Sara as to just where the red hair came from in a marriage between a raven haired woman and a sandy blond haired man. Seth remembered that his mother had once told him that his great grandmother had red hair and he just smiled at the big green eyed, gap toothed, freckled little girl as she ran into his arms.

Seth lifted Kiki into the air and she screamed and laughed with delight. He laid her across his big powerful arms and played airplane with her giving her what she called an airplane ride. Kiki giggled and begged for more. He started to put her down and she grabbed the gold colored wings atop the plentiful decorations on his uniform. Seth tickled Kiki and she let go of the wings. It was a near nightly routine – and Seth wouldn't have taken a million dollars in exchange for it.

Sara had the barbecue started and the family went outside on the back patio. Although it was February, the weather was warm on the beautiful island of Oahu Hawaii. A gentle wind was blowing and the palm trees danced in the fading days light. The smell of barbecued chicken wafted through the air. A large plate in the center of the table was filled with a fresh pineapple, kiwi and bananas. Life was good.

The family sat down to eat and offered thanks to God for their blessings. Seth dished a healthy serving of fruit and chicken on his plate and began to enjoy the meal.

"I had a meeting with Major General Roy Hanes today," Seth said.

Sara looked up from her dinner and smiled.

"What did old Haney want?" she asked.

Seth gave her a reproachful look, although it was he not she who had coined the nickname Old Haney for the Major General.

"Major General Hanes is promoting me," Seth said, stressing Hanes' full title.

"To full bird?" Sara asked gleefully.

"Yes Ma'am, bird Colonel Seth Woodson reporting for duty," he said with a smart salute.

"You don't look like a bird," Kiki complained.

"It means a pay grade advancement Kiki, and that means you might get that bicycle you've been wanting," Seth said. He pulled a pair of silver colored eagle insignia from his pocket and showed them to Kiki and Sara.

Kiki jumped from the table and applauded. She even tried to copy the smart salute she saw her daddy do a moment ago. Seth laughed out loud, hugged her and gave her another airplane ride spin.

"Are we moving or are you going overseas?" Sara asked.

"That's the best part. Base commander, Brigadier General Jason Forrester is retiring and Hanes wants me to take the base," Seth said.

"What about XO Milner?" Sara asked. Sara was asking about Colonel Roger Milner, the man who had served as the Executive Officer for Brigadier General Forrester.

"Milner's accepted an appointment to the Pentagon. He's been promoted to Brigadier General," Seth said.

"Woe, so now you're going to be the Base Commander," Sara said smiling encouragingly.

Seth picked her up and spun her around. "Can you believe it? Hanes said if I keep my nose clean there might even be a Star in it for me," he said. Seth was referring to the possibility of being promoted to Brigadier General at some point in the future.

"Who will be your new XO?" Sara asked.

"The Major General tapped a fellow by the name of Daniel Boyce. He's a Lieutenant Colonel currently stationed in California. He's been ordered to be here Monday the tenth," Seth said.

"Does he have a family?" Sara asked.

Seth pulled a folder from his briefcase, opened it and spent a moment scanning the documents.

"He's married and has a son a year older than Kiki," Seth reported.

Sara smiled at Kiki.

"Daddy and Mommy, can Keiko spend the night this Saturday?" Kiki asked.

Keiko Shibata was a precocious and sassy little girl that had lived next door since a few weeks after Kiki was born. Kiki and Keiko had played together almost everyday of their lives until preschool and now the two seemed to need some time away from the twenty-seven other five and six year olds in their preschool class. Next year, they would be going to first grade together at Barbers Point Elementary school. Keiko's father, Major Ichiro Shibata was a computer programmer and technician.

"I'll call Mrs. Shibata and see, but I don't see any reason why not," Sara said smiling.

The family ate quietly for a few moments.

"I have some news too," Sara said looking up at Seth with dancing eyes.

Seth caught the expression on her face, gasped and nearly choked on a piece of chicken.

He looked at her questioningly with excitement written on his face. Sara smiled merrily.

"The doctor said it's for certain," she said.

Seth stood and took Sara in his arms and Kiki sat looking between the two apprehensively.

"What, Mommy?" Kiki asked.

"Honey, you're going to have a little baby brother or sister!" Sara said.

Kiki was quiet. She wasn't sure she wanted a baby brother or sister. She'd always been the only child and she liked it that way.

Friday, February 7, 2025

Marie Boyce looked up and smiled at her husband Daniel as he walked into the house. She immediately noticed his demeanor and the smile slipped from her lips. The man she often referred to, as dapper Dan looked a bit scruffy tonight.

"Woody, why don't you into your room and play for a while? I think we need a break," she said.

"What's wrong?" Marie asked when their young son Woody was out of earshot.

"I am being transferred. We have to move immediately," Daniel said tossing his Air Force uniform hat onto a nearby chair.

"Where are we going? Or is it just you that's going?" Marie asked.

Daniel sat down, picked up the newspaper and turned to the front page. He looked at it for a moment and then tossed it in a heap onto a nearby table.

"Most guys would consider it gravy duty. We're being sent to Hawaii," Daniel said.

"We both always knew that moving around was part of your career as an Air Force officer," Marie commented.

Daniel didn't look up. He grunted something in her direction and continued brooding. Marie left him in the family room and went to the kitchen.

"I have to catch a hop to Hawaii tomorrow to meet with a recently promoted bird Colonel and a two star General. I'll be working for the new bird under the supervision of the General." Daniel called after her.

Monday, February 10, 2025

Marie was wearing a pair of stylish jeans and a light pink sweater when she saw Daniel off at the base early Monday morning. Her golden hair was up in ponytail and she looked much younger than her thirty-one years. Daniel knew that it was a nearly daily routine that some college-aged boy would wander up to Marie and ask her out. Marie would smile and point to Woody.

"I don't think his daddy would approve," she would say.

Lieutenant Colonel Daniel Boyce stepped from the military aircraft and walked purposely to the waiting jeep. He had left his wife Marie and young son Woody at their house in San Diego while he arranged a place for them to live here at the new duty station in Oahu, Hawaii. He sat briefcase in hand in the back of the jeep and thought of his wife.

The jeep stopped smartly outside of a drab colored military office building and Boyce returned the salute from the enlisted man that served as his driver and marched up the steps and into the building. He was shown to a small comfortable looking office with a view of more drab colored military buildings. Jeeps were coming and going and an occasional group of men and women dressed in military training uniforms marched by. He smiled remembering his own training days and was lost in his own memories when the sound of a man's voice caught his ear.

"Nice view isn't it," Seth said.

Daniel turned around smartly and saluted the Colonel.

"Relax. I was wearing that very uniform just last week," Seth said pointing at the insignia of the Lieutenant Colonel.

Daniel managed a sour looking smile. Seth led Daniel down the beige corridor and into Seth's office.

"Would you like something to drink?" Seth asked pointing to an older model AutoBev400.

"How did you get the brass to spring for that?" Daniel said with an interested smile.

"I didn't. It's mine," Seth said.

"Do they really make over a thousand different types of drinks using only a dozen ingredients?" Daniel asked.

"Nah, this is one of the old ones. They only make about four hundred different drinks, but they still use a dozen ingredients," Seth said.

The AutoBev400 was a machine that had been introduced primarily to restaurants and bars about four-years ago. An old one like Seth had could create a very pleasing reproduction of almost any beverage a person desired using a combination of basic ingredients and flavor substitutes. Seth had gotten this one when a friend of his in the restaurant business had bought the new AutoBev2000 last year. Restaurants and bars had laid off many a bartender and eliminated a lot of waste from what they called over pouring since the new machine came out. Now the bars simply hired minimum wage workers to take the drinks to their patrons. These workers carried a device called a Snuggler strapped to the palm of one hand. The Snuggler was an updated and miniaturized version of the tablet computers popular a decade earlier. Workers entered the customers drink order into the Snuggler along with the table number. The AutoBev2000 received each order wirelessly and made and poured each drink and placed a sheet of clear self-stick Doreum to each glass with the correct table number and drink name. All the server had to do was take the drink to the correct customer.

Doreum was an updated plastic type substance that contains no petroleum products or derivatives. It had been invented in 2022 by Derick M. Covey. Seth had read a magazine article about Covey that indicated Covey had become interested in science after reading a novel in his early teens where one character had amazingly similar attributes to his own. Covey said he more or less 'turned on' his studying side at that point and began to think how an invention like the one he had read about could be done. Covey released Doreum to the public on May 5, 2023, Covey's thirtieth birthday. Covey had of course become an instant celebrity and quickly became a billionaire. It is reported that shortly after he came into his fortune Covey gave his father; a long time truck driver, a brand new truck. Covey gave his mother; a long time homemaker and Boy Scouts of America volunteer, her first brand new car. The article went on to say that Covey was now working on a formula to replace the gasohol mixture that fuels today's vehicles. Covey's new product, yet unnamed, is planned to be a synthetic fuel that does not involve oil. The article concluded suggesting that an article was due shortly about

Mr. Covey's sister, Marie who was about to embark on something spectacular of her own.

Now Seth pushed a few buttons and prepared the cappuccino Daniel had asked for and made himself a café latte. Each drink only took a few seconds to create and each was steaming and delicious. Seth looked at his watch, grabbed his drink and motioned Daniel to do the same. They walked together down more dingy drab halls to a slightly larger office with a small conference table in the center. The Major General was sitting at the table reading a briefing and puffing on a SimCigar. The government had recently banned real cigars and cigarettes after long-time smoker and former president Denton Reams died of lung cancer. Now the SimCigarette and SimCigar trade was rivaling all time tobacco sales records and supposedly without the health risks.

The Major General looked up as Seth and Daniel walked into the room. Daniel stopped to pop to attention and offer a salute and the Major General motioned him to a chair.

"Save it for the public," Major General Hanes said.

"Yes Sir!" Daniel sounded off smartly.

"We're pretty informal in the office. We still do all the military stuff when we are out among the troops or in public, but here in the office its low key," Seth said.

"As long as you don't get too darned low key," The Major General growled chewing the end of his SimCigar. Rings of smoke like light seemed to float from the tip of the SimCigar although it was not burning. The rings came together to form a momentarily visible misty haze reminiscent of those days in years gone by when a room was filled with smoke. But the air remained clean and clear and the effect was only a trick of light.

Seth turned to Daniel and chuckled.

"He's talking about the little nickname I suggested for him," Seth said chuckling.

Daniel looked around uneasily.

"This over paid pencil pusher thinks I'm old," Major General Hanes said sourly as he puffed even more heavily on his SimCigar.

Seth chuckled again.

"I've been known to call him Old Haney," Seth said.

"Don't you go getting any ideas Lieutenant Colonel Boyce," Hanes roared.

Then both Hanes and Seth laughed and Daniel finally started to relax.

Hanes told both Seth and Daniel his expectations during a one-hour meeting and then there was a formal procession to see the Major General off on a helicopter transport to the Honolulu Airport. By this time tomorrow, the Major General would be back in his California office and Seth and Daniel would begin to settle into their new roles.

The World Beyond: The Library on the Other Side

Saturday, March 22, 2025

"Momma, Keiko can't play! She's sick today!" Kiki complained.

"Would you like to go and play with me today?" Sara asked.

Of course Kiki loved the idea. She and Sara set off to a beach area that was primarily used by military families and was far from the tourist hangouts in Waikiki. Sara had brought along a big red and white beach ball, a sand bucket and two towels. Sara wore a simple one-piece bathing suit covered with a pair of denim jean shorts. Kiki was dressed in an identical outfit of her own. They walked along the beachfront frolicking and splashing in the close-in shallow water areas. Sara gently steered Kiki away from any waters that would be higher than the young girl's knees. She and Seth had worked with their next-door neighbors Ichiro and Naoko Shibata to set a time when Keiko and Kiki could attend swim lessons together. But all of that would be in a few months and for now Kiki would have to be gently guided to places on the beach where there was no real danger.

Sara and Kiki were walking to a nice place where they could rest and let the sun dry them when Sara's phone rang. She lifted the phone and saw that it was Seth that was calling. "Just a minute honey, let me tell Kiki where she can play while we talk," Sara said into the phone. Sara put one arm around Kiki and drew an imaginary small circle indicating where the child could play within her sight. Kiki nodded anxiously and ran off towards the far end of the area. Sara smiled at the fact that Kiki always went just a little, not much, but a little further than she was directed to go. Sara of course knew that and always directed the child in a slightly smaller circle than she intended.

Kiki saw a boy about her age playing in the sand maybe ten feet further along the beach. The boy had curly blue-black hair and he was playing with a big green bucket and small blue-green shovel. He wore olive green swim trucks that clashed with his big bright blue eyes. The boy was making strange sounds and scooping up shovel after shovel of sand and pouring each shovel full into the bucket from as far above as he could reach. Kiki walked over to the boy while she noticed his mother lying on a plain white beach towel a few yards away and clad in a multi-colored old-fashioned bathing suit.

"What ya' doin'?" Kiki asked the boy.

He looked up at her and smiled, his big blue eyes sparkling.

"Plantin' a tree," he said. He showed her an acorn and the deep hole he had been digging.

"What's your name?" Kiki asked.

"Woody," he said. "What's yours?"

"Kiki," she said.

Woody gave her a strange look.

"My real name is Leann Liakiki Woodson. Everybody calls me Kiki for short," she said.

"Me too," Woody said nodding.

Now it was Kiki's turn to give Woody a strange look.

"My real name is Lee Woodward Boyce and everybody calls me Woody for short," he said.

The boy pushed his acorn deep into the sand then he stood, brushed sand from his swimsuit, looked at her and extended his hand.

"It's a pleasure to meet you Kiki Woodson," Woody said.

Kiki took his hand and shook it hard. Her daddy said you should always shake a hand hard.

"And it's nice to meet you, Woody Boyce," Kiki said.

"It's funny you and me got sort of the same name. I go by Woody and your last name is Woodson. I'm seven, how old are you?" Woody asked.

"I'm six. I start first grade next year," Kiki said.

"Would you think I'm weird if I told you something?" Woody asked.

"What?" Kiki asked cocking her head to the right.

"If you find yourself on stage at a school play and your best friend is afraid, just start singing," Woody said.

Kiki looked at Woody for a moment and then slowly shook her head.

"Okay," she said.

Woody and Kiki played together and filled the hole Woody had been digging to plant his acorn. When Sara finished her phone call she came over by where the children were playing. Woody's mother got up and came over too.

"Hi," said Sara while shading her eyes from the sun with one hand.

"Hello," said Marie extending a hand.

The two women introduced themselves to each other and made the children go through their introductions over again. Kiki shook Woody's hand even harder this time. Woody smiled toothily.

Sara explained that her husband Seth was the new base commander and Marie explained that her husband Daniel was the new executive officer that Major General Hanes had recruited to assist Sara's husband. The two women shared stories of all the moving; all the months alone while their husbands were away God knew where. They talked about military life and the sense of dread of never knowing when or if their husbands might be called to war. And they talked of the good things like never needing to worry about getting laid off or being without an income. Sara invited Marie and her family to join them for dinner tomorrow and Marie said she would check with Daniel and get back to her. The women and children finally stood, waved goodbye and went their separate ways.

Chapter 18

The Woodson's and the Boyce's enjoyed a great outdoor barbecue and sat around in the small back yard and enjoyed each other's company. It was the first of many such occasions when the families got together. The adults seemed to click and as for the children, well, there was just no doubt that those two were headed for a life long friendship. There seemed to be something almost magic in the children's friendship. After just a few days they seemed like they had known each other all of their lives. They shared a connection that was uncommon and somewhat mysterious.

Later, Sara and Marie would team up to teach Keiko, Woody and Kiki to swim. The mothers would occasionally go swimming or shopping together while the fathers passed several Saturday afternoons playing baseball, football, or volleyball with the children. Sometimes the Shibata's and little Keiko would join the Woodson's and the Boyce's for a day of fun. The relationship between the Woodson's and the Boyce's seemed to keep growing stronger and closer until it was almost as if they were all a part of one big family.

Kiki and Keiko still spent time together. They played all kinds of games like Robotic Family and Hologram Jump rope. Their favorite was the jump-rope game that created huge holographic images of wonderful places. The children could seem to be jumping the Grand Canyon, the Alps and the like.

But it almost seemed that time with Keiko had become secondary to the time Kiki spent with Woody. It was the same with Woody and his best friend Nathaniel.

Time seemed to fly.

Seth and Sara's second child, Doreen, was born September 15, 2025. It was a warm, wet and windy day. Sara had not rushed to the hospital but driven there purposely for a new procedure called Naturally Simple Birth. The procedure involved a process in which a microscopic electronic device had earlier been placed in a strategic location and had monitored Sara's pregnancy. The device notified Sara when to start towards the hospital and also sent moment-by-moment information about Sara's and the baby's condition to the delivery room of the hospital. Seth and Sara had arrived at the hospital at eleven fifteen in the morning and Doreen was born one and one-half hours later. She was a happy, healthy, bald-headed girl with pink cheeks, cherub face and joyful brown eyes.

There were no complications and Sara's total time in labor was seventeen minutes. The ease of her birth was just one more of the medical marvels of the twenty-first century. Seth sat in the Bonding Room with Doreen on his lap. He and Sara had left Kiki with Marie Boyce for the day while Daniel was on duty at the base. Seth gazed at the baby for a while and played with her until she fell asleep. Then he laid her in a nearby crib and picked up a magazine. There was a follow up article on Derick Covey that indicated he had run into a few unexpected complications in creating a truly synthetic fuel for vehicles. Mr. Covey said that the complications represented a delay but not an end to the search for a successful method.

Friday, November 14, 2025

"Kiki, are you ready?" Sara asked.

It was the night of Kiki's first school play. She and Keiko had been secluded in Kiki's room practicing every night for the past week. Kiki had told Sara that Keiko had the key solo at the end of the play. Keiko had been working hard to learn the song. Now the girls burst from Kiki's room. Kiki had one arm around Keiko and seemed to be giving her last minute instructions. The two looked to Sara amazingly like teacher and student except for the fact that both girls were only six years old. Sara smiled and directed the girls to the waiting car.

They arrived at the school and Sara went into the auditorium to save a seat for Seth and Ichiro and Naoko Shibata. Soon the auditorium was filled with excited parents and frazzled teachers. The program was called *'Hawaiian Holly Daze'*. Students from the first to the third grade created the artwork and all the traditional holiday music – together with some decidedly untraditional music was to be performed by the children. A brave third grade boy gave a rousing rendition of the title song, *Hawaiian Holly Daze*. When the tall towheaded lad finished the audience applauded and whistled loudly while they shouting encouragement. Even though the performance wasn't stellar the crowd was pleased by his excellent effort. The audience of parents reacted the same way to almost every child that performed that night. The final curtain opened and two-second graders were caught retreating from pushing a large cardboard set that looked like a smiling globe to the center of the stage. Three six year old girls stood on either side of the globe looking angelic in their long flowing white dresses glimmering in the stage light. Keiko stood a few feet in front of the girls dressed in a beautiful multicolor silk kimono. The recorded background music started and Keiko reached for the microphone. She glanced at Kiki who was standing furthest from her right side and Kiki nodded and smiled. Then the spotlight centered on Keiko and she just froze. After a moment, a teacher walked out to Keiko and said something reassuring. The music was started once again but Keiko remained silent and her fear and discomfort grew rapidly more obvious. The teacher started the music for the third time and Kiki went to stand next to her friend. Keiko pushed the microphone into Kiki's hands and Kiki almost dropped it. Keiko moved behind Kiki as if she could hide there. Kiki took the microphone and offered it to Keiko. Keiko's eyes grew wide and terror was plainly written on her face in the form of a pale white stare.

Then Kiki remembered the strange thing that Woody had said to her when she first met him. He had said that if she found herself on stage and her best friend was afraid that Kiki should just start singing. So Kiki turned to the audience and began to sing.

The audience went stone cold silent. Parents and teachers jaws dropped visibly. Sara sat unconsciously dabbing at the stream of tears from her eyes. Her expression shifted from shock to amazement then she lifted her head, her face still moist with tears and beaming with pure parental pride. Seth, who moments earlier had sat with his long legs crossed and quietly conversing with Ichiro now sat flatfooted and ram rod straight in a position of full military attention. His carefully trained facial expression revealing nothing. Naoko, who had started to stand and go to Keiko, was stopped by Ichiro's hand at Kiki's first note. Now the two sat quietly together, holding hands, heads bowed as if in prayer. The teacher that had been on the way to take the microphone stopped mid-step and remained there as if frozen in her tracks. Goose bumps were obvious on both of her long thin arms and tears streamed down her cheeks.

Kiki was oblivious to it all and she just kept singing *What a Wonderful World.* The other children were supposed to come in on the second verse. There was a key change that they had practiced time and time again – but the other children remained silent. Kiki didn't seem to notice. She took the key change like she had been doing it for years and she poured even more heart and passion into the song. She allowed herself to relax and enjoy the songs simple beauty and then she stretched and hit a powerful high note as the song ended.

Silence rained on the audience like a forest of trees shedding leaves after a fall windstorm. Kiki placed the microphone on the stand and turned her back to walk away. First a few people started quietly applauding and then real applause burst from the audience. This was not the sound of parents wishing to make a child feel accepted; this was the honest sincere applause of an audience that had been treated to a major musical miracle. Kiki had brought down the house.

Her voice had been so powerful, so rich, and so full of feeling and beauty that no one had been able to believe such a voice could come from a six-year-old child. But the voice had come, and it had left them all with a piece of their hearts swimming in the ecstasy of the unexpected professional level singing performance. Now the crowd was on their feet, stomping and applauding and cajoling Kiki to return to the microphone. Kiki took Keiko's hand and brought her friend back to the front and the two girls took a bow together. But the audience would not stop. They demanded another song, or at least that Kiki sing the same song again just so that they could verify that they had truly heard such a thing and that it had not all been a dream. Keiko picked up the microphone and handed it to Kiki. Kiki smiled at the audience and took up the last verse of the song again as the background music played. At her first note the audience was instantly silent, instantly enraptured and instantly enthralled. Kiki finished the song and left the stage to yet another rousing standing ovation. Kiki returned to stage one last time. This time, she sang not a word but blew the audience a kiss and quietly spoke these four words; "It's all in you." She said pointing to the audience from left to right. And a brand new singing legend was born.

2025- 2035

On Christmas Eve 2025 Seth and Sara gave Kiki and Doreen a puppy. The puppy was an adorable female golden retriever with expressive big brown eyes and the girls were immediately in love with her. The girls decided to name the puppy Lynn. And for a long while, the girls and the puppy were inseparable. By early January 2026, Kiki had begun professional level voice lessons from a well-known Hollywood voice instructor named Macy Peabody Boyle.

The years ticked by like the rushing sound of a ruthless wave. Kiki sang at school and at church from 2027 to 2028. In the late summer of 2029 she was invited to sing with the Honolulu Symphony. During holiday school break of 2029 she was invited to sing with the New York Philharmonic and in the summer of 2030 she toured with the Boston Pops. In 2031 and 2032 she performed with other child prodigies. She performed alongside well-known big name artists. In 2033 she opened the retirement concerts of formerly famous artist Nikki Clearson. All through the years there were times she spent with Keiko and times she spent with Woody. There were times when she went to school like any girl her age and times when Kiki had a private tutor. There were times spent with Macy Boyle and times when her family and friends flew thousands of miles to be at Kiki's performances. Nearly every time that Kiki stepped on stage an odd silence swept the audience until she had sung her last note. Nearly every time she stood for curtain call after curtain call and each time she came back on stage for one last silently blown kiss to the audience and her now famous words spoken and echoed by the audience.

"It's all in you," Kiki would say and the audience would roar back the same words to her as she left the stage with the crowds still begging for more.

In early 2034 when Kiki was only fifteen, she won the Overall Best-Selling Recording Artist award. She had won so many other awards that she could keep only a few. 2035 was the first year she had best selling albums in three different genres; pop, country and jazz.

Life had been adventurous for Woody too. In early fall 2029 Woody awoke to find a ten-foot-tall angel standing at the foot of his bed. Woody had not panicked or been afraid; it was as if he had almost expected this visitor.

"I need a healing angel today," He casually told the big angel.

The big angel had smiled, nodded his head and disappeared. Woody walked downstairs and greeted his mother with an unusual request.

"I would like to go visit the base hospital today. I especially want to visit the sick children," he said.

Marie Boyce smiled at Woody. "How sweet! What made you think of such a thing?" she asked.

"I don't know I just have a feeling I should go visit them today," Woody said.

They drove together to the base hospital in silence and walked to the children's care unit. Woody stood in the exact center of the hallway holding both arms rigidly out to each side. Then he simply began walking down the hall. Marie Boyce was unsure what Woody was doing but no one was complaining so she let him continue. He had past the third or fourth set of doors when a commotion came from both sides of the aisle behind them. The little boy on the west side of the hall had broken both his legs and one arm in a sporting accident, and now the boy was up out of bed walking around as good as new. The girl on the east side of the hall had been suffering from extreme respiratory failure as a result of severe asthma. She was now insisting that she could breathe perfectly.

The further down the hall Woody walked the more the phenomena spread; a child with cancer began instantaneous remission, a child with a large misshapen head was suddenly normal, and more and more and more. When Wally came to the end of the hall he collapsed in exhaustion. By now every doctor and nurse on the wing was busy trying to figure out what was happening and Marie simply went to Woody; picked him up and quietly walked away from the hospital wing. A few days later she asked Woody how he had done this and he replied in the simple truth of an eleven-year old child. "I didn't do it. All I had to do was to keep believing. The healing angel did it."

Every three months Woody would awake and make the same request of an angel he found standing at the foot of his bed and each time Woody would ask to visit sick people in hospitals all over Oahu. Every time people would mysteriously get well and yet Woody's involvement remained a secret until the middle of the third year.

One day Woody had followed his usual practice of asking to visit a particular group of patients at a particular hospital. When he and his mother arrived that day, Woody noticed a young boy lying in a hospital bed just outside the hospital entrance. A catholic priest dressed in full regalia stood at the head of the bed reciting the boy's last rights. The boy's mother stood dressed in black from head to toe and crying miserably. Almost without thinking Woody raised a hand toward the boy and in that instant Woody's life changed forever. Instantaneously, the boy began to cough and sat up in bed. The boy pushed the oxygen mask away from his face and a broad smile appeared on his face. The boy's face gleamed with energy and vitality. Doctors responded in shock and one nurse that had seen it all began to whisper that Woody had done something to heal the boy. The place became a buzz as the young boy climbed from his bed and began telling his mother that he was hungry. The color had returned to the boy's face and he looked the picture of health. The boy's physician examined him and found him to be without any type of ailment. The boy's heart was now in perfect condition and the physician had no explanation as to how that could have happened.

The story was on the news that night and in the morning addition of the newspaper the following morning. Calls and letters begging Woody to come heal people began to pour in from all corners of the world. For a while, Woody and his parents traveled and hundreds of seriously ill people were miraculously healed. The family accepted only enough to finance the travel. Then a billionaire from the Middle East called and offered any sum of money for Woody to come and heal him and Woody refused. The press called Woody a racist, a terrorist and a traitor to his country because he would not go to heal the man. Finally, a high placed government official stepped in and mandated that Woody go and heal the billionaire. But Woody was unsuccessful in his attempt and he lost the support of the public in that failure, and possibly saved his own life in the process.

In 2036, the year that Kiki was sixteen, her world fell apart. It began when her best friend Keiko and her family were suddenly transferred and had to move almost without notice. Keiko's father, Ichiro Shibata was a military man, and military men were occasionally moved by powers that they did not see and superior officers that they did not know. Major Shibata, a computer systems genius, had been offered a promotion to Lieutenant Colonel. The term sounded much better than it actually was, because although it was couched as an offer it was actually an order. The promotion carried with it a move back to the mainland and within a few short days the place that had one housed Kiki's best friend was vacant and to Kiki it looked somehow smaller now. She could of course still video chat with her friend over the net but it wouldn't be the same.

Keiko moving away was only the beginning of Kiki's worst year. She had recently returned from a week long concert in New York City and she found Woody sitting in the school cafeteria with Marjorie Marley, a leggy and popular blond with sparkling ice blue eyes, a too tight blouse and too short cut off jeans. The two looked way to friendly to Kiki and she was hurt and angry with Woody. Woody tried to explain and he reminded Kiki that he had told her that Keiko would soon be forced to move away. He told Kiki that Marjorie was just a friend but seeing the two together Kiki didn't see it that way. When Woody tried to warn Kiki not to spend a day in the park with her younger sister, an opportunity that seldom presented itself, the pressure between the two of them became too strong and the two kindred spirits went each their own way. Shortly afterward the worst day of Kiki's young life unfolded.

Paul L. Bailey

February 27, 2036

Wednesday was a teacher-planning day and there was no school. It was a warm day spotted with several short downpours of rapid rain and a few clouds skating across the cerulean sky. A gentle wind stirred thick green blades of grass. Kiki and her ten-year-old sister Doreen were spending a peaceful day on the North Shore of Oahu walking their dog Lynn through the newly restored Haleiwa Park.

The word Haleiwa means *House of the Iwa.* It is named for a beautiful bird that embodies the beauty of the North Shore of the Island. Decades ago Haleiwa was set in the middle of nowhere but now this beautiful area was where the newest hotels and resorts and the new center of commerce for Oahu. The beaches at Waikiki, which had long been tourists stomping grounds had fallen into disrepair and tourists, were beginning to go elsewhere by early 2028. The once quiet North Shore had begun a revitalization project that had tourists begging to pay the exorbitant prices for a luxurious and peaceful time away from battered Waikiki and Diamond Head.

Kiki was dressed in a white Hawaiian Kimono, a black wig and oversized sunglasses under a wide straw hat while Doreen was wearing a simple bathing suit with a tank top cover. The park contained a single roughly elliptical wandering path that crossed several faux wooden bridges gapping a man made riverbed stocked with Kohaku, Butterfly Koi and Goldfish. Lazy butterflies fluttered through the air creating a colorful and relaxing atmosphere. Lynn sniffed curiously at a bare patch of ground and then raised her furry head to Doreen. Lynn was usually slow and methodical but today she seemed excited and began pulling at her virtual leash. The virtual leash was an invention that allowed a dog to run free while simultaneously being under remote control. The application allowed pet owners virtually the same control, as they would have with the old style leash and from any distance of up to one mile. It was clear that Lynn wanted to run and play and although it seemed curious to Doreen for Lynn to act this way, Doreen put the leash on extended area and allowed Lynn to run. It was unusual for Kiki and Doreen to have an entire day to spend together since Kiki was constantly going off to perform at one event or another. Doreen adored her older sister and was sometimes jealous of her success.

"It's not fair. You have all the talent," Doreen complained.

"Believe me, I'd give it to you if I could," Kiki said.

Kiki looked down at the grass then back into Doreen's light blue eyes.

"Actually, I guess I wouldn't give it to you. But it's not because it's a good thing. It's because sometimes it's a terrible thing," Kiki said.

"How can it be terrible to be the most popular teenage singing star in the United States and maybe even in the whole world?" Doreen asked.

"That's just it. I'm not Kiki, the person. I'm always 'the American young superstar singing sensation Leann Woodson.' I don't get time off to just be a teenage kid. I even have to wear a disguise just to go to the park with my little sister," Kiki said pointing to her bizarre outfit.

Doreen looked at Kiki with an expression of wonder.

"I'd like to just have one normal day. One day that no one would recognize me and start screaming, no one would scream my name in a crowded mall or and no one would gasp as I walk past, " Kiki said.

"Normal isn't everything it's cracked up to be," Doreen said with a grimace.

Kiki put an arm around Doreen's shoulder. "Neither is being a superstar," she said quietly.

The girls walked together silently for several moments. Kiki noticed a maroon four-door sedan slowing to a crawl and cruising by on Pilikia Avenue as if looking for someone. The sedans brakes squeaked and the motor sounded out of sorts. Kiki glanced up at the vehicle and wondered if she had been spotted in spite of her disguise. The car continued rolling slowly by and Kiki relaxed a bit. In the center of the park was a children's play area containing swings, slides and a merry-go-round. Three little girls wearing multicolored bathing suits were covered in sand and laughing while they took turns pushing each other on the swings. Two young boys played with toy trucks in a sand box and Kiki momentarily glanced at the boys and remembered the day she and Woody had tried to plant an acorn in the sand near the ocean.

A mother walked around the play area behind a self-propelled stroller containing a bald two-year-old child that might have been either male or female. She had programmed her smartphone and set a path for the stroller to follow her and to match her pace. Lynn looked up from her romp in the park, ears peaked and she began a low growl and a slow walk toward the nearby car. As she grew closer the dog bared her teeth and barked several sharp warnings before returning to her low growl. Her head moved down and her tail stood high and tight. Doreen turned toward the dog and fumbled with her phone and it fell to the ground. A rubber-like substance protected the device and it was not damaged, but it took Doreen a moment to retrieve it. Kiki placed her hands near her mouth and loudly called to Lynn. Lynn ignored her and continued, moving faster now, toward the slow moving car. Doreen accessed the virtual leash program on her PCED and gave Lynn's leash a strong virtual pull. The dog turned and looked at Doreen accusingly and then began moving even more quickly towards the car. The car's driver apparently saw the dog and first came to a complete stop then started again and sped up slightly. Both Kiki and Doreen were now running towards the dog. Doreen was easily outdistancing her older sister. Doreen was used to running and playing while Kiki was more used to concert performances and autograph sessions. Lynn took a cross-country path and quickly closed the distance to the car. The closer the dog came to the car the fiercer her growl became. The car began to swerve erratically and once again slowed its pace. Now nearly at the car, the dog leaped as if to attack it and instead landed directly in front of it. Lynn started to move towards the driver's side when the car suddenly accelerated and intentionally steered toward her. Lynn set her body to jump out of the way, but the car was too fast. Doreen was only a few feet behind the dog when she saw her leap into the roadway. She stared unbelievingly as the car turned toward the dog and deliberately hit her. Doreen heard a single yelp from Lynn followed by a sickening crunch. Doreen stopped in her tracks and then turned toward the car. She could not abide looking at the remains of her mangled pet. Her anger and grief merged and her face flushed in indignation.

A gray haired gaunt man in tattered blue jeans and no shirt jumped from the car. Doreen rushed at him, her index finger shaking and pointing. She began to berate the man with a litany of accusations and curses. The man simply stood there and allowed Doreen to get as close as she liked. When she had closed the distance, the man grabbed her hand by the pointing finger and drew Doreen toward him. Kiki stopped and screamed with the full force of her powerful voice.

First she screamed, "Someone Help!" then she screamed at the man, "Stop! Let her go!"

It was a thunderous sound, menacing but still somehow melodious. Doreen was struggling to fight off the man until he pushed the base of his large hand into Doreen's midsection and Kiki watched in terror as Doreen deflated like a burst balloon. Kiki stopped running and hit the emergency pad on her phone. Within seconds the device would send her exact global position to the police. It would also begin transmitting full circle video from around Kiki. The man threw Doreen over his shoulder and tossed her carelessly into the open back seat of the sedan. Doreen was wheezing and gasping for breath. The man slammed the car door and crawled through the passenger side. Sirens had already started to wail. The man pulled himself behind the steering wheel; reached across and pulled the passenger door closed, and hit the accelerator. The car shot forward and quickly sped away. Kiki stood there a moment out of breath and shaking in silent shock. Then the police were there and the horrible reality that Doreen was gone and that Lynn was dead began to sink in.

Seth and Sara were convinced that the incident had been a kidnapping. They figured someone knew that Doreen was Kiki's little sister and that the kidnappers wanted some of the money Kiki was earning with her musical talent. In exchange for Doreen's life – they would have happily given it to them. The following day, police found the car abandoned and wiped clean of fingerprints. The car had belonged to a family that owned a vacation home on the Island. The family kept the old car to serve them during their visits. Since they were temporarily on the mainland, they had no idea the car had been stolen.

Searches were fruitlessly conducted. Kiki had given the police a detailed description of the man, but even with the transmitted footage from her phone, no known suspects were located. Kiki looked through several pages of mug shots – but saw no one that vaguely resembled the gray haired man.

For months no other clues to Doreen's whereabouts were discovered. Then one day almost a year after the incident a tourist found the remains of Doreen's body buried in a shallow grave.

Slowly, painfully, and with much grief and guilt, life went on and time passed.

Paul L. Bailey

Sunday, March 29, 2037

Kiki walked quietly into the house just after five in the morning. She had just returned from a three-day concert in Rochester. Her newest album was number one on the music charts and her concerts were sold out weeks before she ever arrived at a location. Kiki sighed. She carried her small overnight case into her bedroom and pushed the door closed. The delivery service would bring the remainder of her wardrobe later in the day. Kiki took a long leisurely shower, dressed in a pair of cut off jeans and a simple top, and flopped flat on her back onto the bed, her arms spread wide. An errant string of red hair fell across Kiki's face and she tried to blow it away puffing out her cheeks. Finally, she pushed the strand away with her hand and sat up and looked out her bedroom window. An orange colored moving truck was parked in front of the house next door where Keiko used to live. Memories of childhood flooded Kiki's thoughts. She had lost contact with Keiko although at first the girls had talked on the phone, emailed and chatted with each other online. Then the concerts began in earnest, and Kiki was always busy. Kiki wondered for a moment where Keiko was now and then peeked from her window curiously at the moving truck.

A military officer in civilian clothing stood speaking with the driver of the truck. A tiny brown dog with white marking on the paws that looked like socks stood with his head tilted up at the two men. A woman about Kiki's mother's age came out from inside the house and stood with her arms crossed looking at the two men chatting. She was wearing a beige heavy looking knee length dress that was obviously not purchased for Hawaii's weather.

A tall blond haired boy about Kiki's age came out of the house and walked toward the moving truck. His eyes perfectly matched the faded blue jeans and hunter style shirt he wore. Kiki smiled to herself. The family looked as if they had just moved from a place where late March might still bring snow. The boy was very masculine and Kiki smiled at that too. Then she sighed again, no time for romance in the life of a young singer. There were too many concerts and too many recording sessions. Isn't that why Woody had abandoned her for that blond leggy Marjorie Marley?

Kiki let the curtain fall back into place and walked back to her desk and sat down. A moment later there was a knock but it did not come from the front door- but rather from Kiki's window frame. She stood, walked to the curtain and opened it. The tall blond boy stood there a big smile pasted on his face. He spoke with a definite mid-west accent but Kiki thought it was cute.

"Hi there ma' names Wally. Was' yours?" he said.

Kiki smiled because the boy hadn't asked for an autograph or anything. In fact he didn't seem to know who she was. "My name is Leann Woodson," Kiki said. She was using both her real name and the stage name by which she was known by her fans. She used it to see how this boy Wally would react.

Wally just smiled. "Very nice to make your ac-cointance, Ms. Woodson," he said.

Now Kiki's smile was even wider. He didn't know who she was! How cool was that!

"Ma family's movin' nex-store –n I jus' wan-ed ta inter-duce ma-self." Wally said smiling. He put out a big hand and offered it to Kiki. Kiki shook it.

The World Beyond: The Library on the Other Side

2037-2039

Kiki and Wally became quick friends. It was as if somehow she had known and cared for him before and their friendship was almost magic. She wasn't surprised when Wally asked her if she would like to go with him to a movie. She went, and the two had a great time. Wally never mentioned the disguise Kiki was wearing. It was almost as if he didn't notice and it wasn't long before Wally and Kiki were going out at least once a week when Kiki wasn't traveling. Wally always went to the airport to see Kiki off when she left to go to a concert, and he was always there to welcome her back when she returned.

Friendship gave way to romance. It was almost as if the times apart didn't exist for either of them. They were like a dream, a different world. When those times were over, Kiki and Wally were together again and it was as if they had never been apart.

Woody noticed and tried, unsuccessfully, to win Kiki back. Woody and Marjorie had never really dated but Woody still made it clear to everyone that he and she had split up. Marjorie was now dating one of the football players from Brigham Young University.

Time passed.

Then one day Kiki met a Wally she had not known. She saw him bullying a seemingly helpless younger student just outside the schoolyard. Wally pushed the boy and taunted him until Kiki was close enough to call out.

"Stop it Wally," she yelled.

Wally turned and looked her direction but his face did not reflect remorse. Instead, he seemed to taunt her now. Wally's eyes were full of a hatred that drove the fondness Kiki had once held for him far away.

"This is none of your business, Woodson," Wally said with a sardonic smirk.

Several other boys arrived at the scene and Wally stormed away in a huff. It was shortly after that incident that Kiki realized that what she had felt for Wally was only a misplaced friendship. By the beginning of summer 2039 Kiki and Woody were back together and on an early spring Sunday morning in 2040 Kiki and Woody were married in a tiny church that stood atop a hill. It was as if they both had known it would happen almost since they first met on the beach in their early childhood. They enjoyed a week vacationing in a country setting in rural Vermont and they both managed to stay out of the headlines for a few weeks.

Chapter 19

Woody and Kiki lived the remainder of their life in joy although they also lived among various clouds of worry and doubt. Kiki went on singing well into her late fifties and all of that time Woody went on helping, healing and teaching those who were willing. The couple never lacked money but they never accumulated the wealth that some would associate with success because every time they had more than they needed; they gave it to those who were truly in need.

The couple retired in their early sixties and spent the next twenty years laughing and loving the remnants of their lives. Then on a sunny Sunday morning in 2105 Woody asked Kiki to go for a walk with him. It was not uncommon for the couple to walk together hand-in-hand on the beaches, but today, Woody and Kiki took a taxi to the tiny beach where they had met as children. The military base had long since been closed and houses and apartments dotted the once serene setting. Despite the sounds of hurry and the never-ending series of vacationer arrivals and departures, the beach itself retained its splendor.

Woody and Kiki walked slowly along the beach until they came upon an unusual sight. There, standing maybe two hundred feet from the waters edge stood a large and impressive oak tree. Woody turned to Kiki and smiled.

"You don't suppose," he asked.

Kiki smiled. "You're such a romantic. Of course it couldn't be," she said.

No matter if it could be or not, the mighty oak stood precisely in the spot that Woody and Kiki had once worked together as children to plant an acorn. Now Woody motioned to Kiki and the couple sat down in the shade of the big tree to rest for a while. The lulling sounds of a seagulls cry together with the gentle breeze and the rustling of the leaves set a peaceful tone. Ocean waves quietly crashed in the distance and in the tranquility around them Kiki and Woody held hands as they fell fast asleep.

Two hours later a passerby noticed the couple lying under the tree and tried to rouse them. There was no rousing them. The two had drifted off the face of the planet and into the peaceful garden on the Other Side.

Chapter 20

We stand here now in the garden and we simultaneously stand in the City of Glass. We watch, now dressed in bodies similar to those we had in our early thirties, as a lone police officer stands in his dark blue uniform calling a medical examiner. We see our discarded and aged bodies lying softly under the oak tree and still holding hands. We join our spirit hands now and look into each other's spirit eyes. Now our eyes are silver and our gowns a glowing white.

Officer Steven Prichard turned away from our bodies and continued reporting our Earthly demise.

"Say again?" said the squeaky voice transmitted by the tiny speaker of the mini phone.

"Former singing sensation Leann Woodson and her husband, the famous healer and teacher Lee Woodward Boyce have been found dead under an oak tree on the beach," Officer Pritchard said.

"I got the part about Woodson and Boyce, but did you say there is an oak tree on the beach?" The voice asked.

In obvious frustration Officer Pritchard spun around to face our bodies as if to confirm the presence of the oak tree but in that moment the oak tree vanished and David smiled with excitement. His task was now completed.

"Uhh, forget the part about the tree. I must be getting too old for this job. I could have sworn there was a big oak tree right there on the beach in Honolulu. What was in my morning coffee?" Pritchard asked.

***

"Woody and I walked hand-in-hand through the garden. This time, because of Woody's gift, our Earthly exit took neither of us by surprise. We knew the day was coming and we knew our missions had been accomplished. Woody's gift allowed us to remember in our final moments all the truth of our previous Visits. Now we turned the final corner of the garden and saw the path that leads to the library on our right and another path to our left. This path had seemed grayed out the last time we had been here but now it was open and available to us. Woody took my hand and we started down the path – but I stopped and turned around. Joan and Mark, Woody's and my Spirit Guides were instantly at our sides. I resolutely turned around and Woody and I returned to the City of Glass."

"During our lives we learned many lessons including that it is impossible to fail in life. We learned that you arrive at your future, what is behind you is not your failure – it is your past. Spell past in a different way and you get 'passed.' It is a clue to the reality that life is not a test that you can fail – you can only pass. The beauty of what we once called the past is laid before us as a testament to the reality of what the bright light before us contains. A new path and a new process are before us and we welcome it and know that whatever it contains is for our greatest good and the greatest good of others. We are fully aware that we now transition to another wheel or another spoke upon the same wheel, but we have no cause for fear or dismay. The path before us is lighted by the truth of what we have learned and the certain knowledge that there is more to learn. The path is made more familiar by knowing who we truly are and yet illuminated the path is not without pleasure. The new path before us is yet another story and perhaps we shall have the opportunity to share that story in some future day on Earth."

"We have shared these stories and these truths with you. You may call us Leena, Lucretia, Leann, Kiki, Lee, Edward or Woody. It is we who pause and offer you this gift. Although we are willing go where Joan and Mark lead us, we leave you this legacy of truth."

"You have heard the truth and you know at least one way to understand an answer to life's most interesting questions. Now, just before the door between us is locked, just before it disappears into the endless life and limitless expanse of the Source, we call with our loudest voice of silent thought, our hands reaching out to you, our spirits soaring. We call with hope and longing to bridge the gap between where we stand on the Other Side to where you stand on Earth and we implore you to consider your life. Don't you know how important you are? You are the only being in all of creation, past, present or future, that experiences things just as you do. You are so very important!"

"Know that you are loved. Know that you are – more. We feel the tug of Joan and Mark and we must go. Do not fear what you call death. Do not be in awe of what you call life after death. Know that every person who you have ever loved and that have gone on before you is waiting for you. You! They are aware that you imagine that they are gone but they are not gone. They are only on the Other Side. We join together with one voice and call to you one last time."

" It's all in you!"

About the Author

Paul L. Bailey lives in Lake Havasu City, Arizona with his wife April and dachshund Roxie. Paul is a member of the Lake Havasu City Writers Group (www.LHCWriters.com) where he serves as president.

A lover of technology, Paul's goal is to eventually link writers groups across the United States to gain better acceptance for self published books by major retailers.

Paul is a former member of Toastmasters International where he earned the title of Distinguished Toastmaster.

Learn more about Paul and his other books at his website, www.PaulBaileyBooks.com.

Paul L. Bailey

You've read the novel, "The World Beyond." Now it's time to enjoy an easy-to-read workbook that will help you meet your Spirit Guide and work through your own views of things here on Earth and the World Beyond.

Paul's Other Books Include:

"Fate's Knight,"a Fantasy Fiction novel
"Knight Fall,"the sequel to "Fate's Knight"
"Weird Stuff," a collection of unusual short stories.
"How to Publish Your Book Free," a step-by-step guide to saving hundreds if not thousands of dollars by publishing your book free.

Most of Paul's books are available on Amazon.com, on Kindle, and at his website.
www.PaulBaileyBooks.com